MEIKE ZIERVOGEL is the founder and director of an award-winning UK publishing house. She was brought up in Northern Germany. After studying Arabic she worked as a journalist for Agence France-Press and Reuters. She lives in London with her husband and two children.

Magda

MEIKE ZIERVOGEL

SALT

CROMER

PUBLISHED BY SALT PUBLISHING
12 Norwich Road, Cromer, Norfolk NR27 0AX United Kingdom

First published by Salt Publishing, 2013

Printed in Great Britain by Clays Ltd, St Ives plc

Typeset in Paperback 9.5/14.5

ISBN 978 1 907773 40 2 paperback

3 5 7 9 8 6 4 2

CONTENTS

Magda

THE PREPARATION

Magda enters Joseph's study without knocking. Joseph is pacing back and forth between fireplace and chaise-longue, hands clasped behind his back, slightly bent forward. He doesn't stop when his wife comes in. Magda crosses the room, sits down at the desk, pulls paper, pen and ink towards her and begins to write. When she has finished she takes some banknotes out of the top drawer and divides them calmly between three envelopes, which she then seals with the letters inside. Joseph is still pacing up and down. They know what to do; he can rely on his wife.

She leaves the room with the letters in her hand. The cook in the kitchen is the first. Magda gives her the envelope. 'Your service was greatly appreciated, but we don't need you any longer.'

'Madam, please don't act too rashly,' the cook pleads, taking two steps towards her mistress. 'There are surely other ways.'

A strict mistress, that's what she's been all these years, but to her – Bertha – always fair. Having now lived side by side for so many years and seen their shared dream fall to pieces, surely a bit of fellow feeling would be welcome. But Magda stares expressionless at her.

'Bertha, pull yourself together. You will leave the house in half an hour.'

With the gardener and Joseph's chauffeur it is easier, less emotional. They, too, receive their envelopes, in which they will find more than enough; it will last them at least a few months. Decent compensation. May they be happy.

After the task is completed, Magda sits down at the big kitchen table and smokes a cigarette. Then she rings the bell that hangs next to the kitchen door, a sign for the children to gather. And here they come already, racing down the stairs, led by Helmut, her nine-year-old boy, so thin and frail and anaemic he looks barely seven. He is dressed up as a Red Indian. An Indian chief, judging by his impressive headdress with red-, green- and blue-dyed pheasant feathers. He wears a loincloth over his cropped trousers and carries a tomahawk in one hand. Karl, Joseph's chauffeur, made him this Indian outfit. Holde, Hedda and Heide, the three little ones, are right on their brother's heels. Holde and Hedda sit down next to Helmut on the bench, one on either side, and four-year-old Heide climbs onto his lap. They sit very still, observing their mother silently. They are used to seeing Bertha during the day, especially in the kitchen; their mother, if at all, appears only at dinner. Eventually Hilde, the eleven-year-old, shuffles through the door and onto the bench. Magda smiles at her five little darlings, waiting for the last one, the eldest. She wonders if Helga has already come down the stairs and is now standing in the corridor behind the door.

'Helga,' Magda calls. Then again, 'Heeelga!' No answer.

'You can come in and sit down with us,' Magda says into the silence.

Holde giggles.

Helmut pinches his sister's arm. 'Be quiet!'

'Do you know where Helga is?' Magda asks her youngest.

Heide shakes her head, lips closed tightly.

'Well –' Magda raises her voice – 'I am sure Helga will hear us, wherever she may be.'

And Magda can feel her daughter's gaze on her back. Quickly she turns her head. Hears the kitchen clock ticking. She looks again at the children.

'We are going on a long journey.'

Five pairs of children's eyes are firmly fixed on her mouth. They don't burst out in cheers; they don't seem to be happy. Instead they throw sceptical glances at their mother.

'Is Father coming?' Helmut finally asks.

Magda nods. 'Yes, Father will come too. It's a family outing.'

'A family outing to Uncle Adolf's house in the mountains, like we used to do?' enquires Holde. She likes Uncle Adolf, that grumpy old man in his big house. They were allowed to have biscuits in his kitchen whenever they wanted.

'We might pass Uncle Adolf's house,' replies Magda. 'But we are going further this time.'

'To where?' asks Helmut, keeping a close eye on his mother, as if slightly suspicious.

'It's an adventure.' Magda hesitates, suddenly wondering how best to explain it to the children. 'We are going on an adventure just like the white settlers leaving for America. Bound for the Wild West.'

'But I am not a white settler.' Helmut interrupts his mother indignantly. 'I am a Red Indian. A Red Indian chief. And these are my squaws. If you are a white settler, you will kill us.'

'Indians don't die, they go to the happy hunting grounds,' Magda reassures her son.

The answer appears to satisfy Helmut.

'Do we have to pack a lot? And will there be horses we can ride?' Heide is suddenly perking up.

'You don't have to pack anything. We can't take much. You are allowed only one toy each. You'll have a nice hot bath tonight and I'll put out clean nightclothes for all of you. You have to have a good night's rest. And so that you sleep really well, you are all allowed a cup of hot milk with honey in bed.'

'Oh!' Heide claps her hands together excitedly. 'Like when we are sick.'

'That's right. And tomorrow we'll drive to Berlin, to Uncle Adolf's bunker, where we might stay a few days. Then we'll go on.'

'But what about the Russians? I thought they'd surrounded us.'

Helmut holds his tomahawk aloft, gripping it tightly.

'The Russians?' Magda smiles, shrugging her shoulders casually. 'The army has driven them back.'

'Is that why Father is home? Because we've won the war?'

'Yes, my darling, because we've won the war, that's right.'

'That's not true.'

Helga has suddenly appeared in the door. No one heard her coming or noticed her standing there.

'We've lost the war,' Helga cries. 'And Uncle Adolf is dead.'

Magda squints, focusing on her daughter. But before she has time to reply, they hear Joseph's voice.

'We have won the war, defeated the enemy and the Führer is alive and well.'

His silhouette appears behind Helga in the half-shadow of the hallway. He takes another step forward and places his hands slowly on his daughter's shoulders, turning her around to face him. Then he lifts one hand as if to slap her across the face. Helga flinches, evading her father's eyes.

'Such lies will never come out of your mouth again. Is that clear?' His voice trembles, his hand hanging in mid-air is shaking.

Helga does not look up. She perceives the raised hand out of the corner of her eye. Father has never hit her, never even come close to it.

'What are you going to do with us?' she whispers.

'We are going on an adventure,' shouts Heide.

'There you are. Listen to your little sister,' Joseph replies. He lowers his hand, only to raise it abruptly again and – almost an afterthought – gently strokes his eldest daughter's cheek before turning around towards the staircase. Slowly he starts to climb the steps.

THE GIRL BEHIND THE CONVENT WALLS

She sinks down to the ground, her eyes on the wooden Virgin Mary and under her knees the cold stone tiles of the old chapel. She shivers and doesn't know anything about God, even if the nuns talk about him all the time. She cannot see God, therefore he doesn't exist. And anyway she doesn't really believe that Mary got pregnant with Jesus just like that. She's observed things quite differently with the dogs. The harsh material of her grey dress itches and she no longer feels her two little toes, but she knows it's no use crying because her mother ... Yes, it's actually from her mother that Magda learnt how Mary got pregnant with Jesus. She'd seen her mother through the half-closed door and heard her, and heard the man too. It didn't look nice, with his bum going up and down and her mother screaming for more. And then a few weeks later ... The man had visited a number of times, but Magda didn't spy on them again, since it wasn't a pretty sight. Also there was the man's groaning and the suppressed squealing of her mother, like a pig. No, not nice at all. So, a few weeks after the first time, the man stayed away and a woman came instead, again late in the evening, when her mother believed Magda to be asleep. But Magda wasn't. The woman disappeared with a bag into the bedroom. Soon afterwards her mother started screaming again, only this time she was definitely screaming for it to stop, not for more. The downstairs neighbour, Egon Müller, knocked on the ceiling with a broom. Fear nailed Magda to the bed. Her mother had told her never to interfere. When the screaming finally stopped, Magda heard the woman talk in a calm voice and shortly afterwards her mother's bedroom door creaked. Magda jumped out of bed. In the hallway she met the woman, who had an enamel bowl in her hands, and the bowl was filled with a bloody lump.

'Is my mother dead now?'

'No, not at all. She's just a silly woman, that's all.'

'And what's this?' Magda pointed to the bowl.

'It's something you don't understand yet.'

But Magda understood. And Egon Müller's son from downstairs helped her to understand even more. It was from him that Magda learnt the full truth about the story of Mary and the Holy Spirit and Jesus. Mary got pregnant because of Joseph: his naked bum moved up and down, and perhaps she squealed like her mother and screamed for more, or kept still like the bitch when the dog puts it in from behind. That, too, Magda observed very closely indeed, because Egon Müller's son told her, 'See what the dogs are doing over there? Adults do the same. But it looks nicer with dogs,' he went on, explaining, 'They do it better and the bitch keeps beautifully still.' Egon Müller's son was particularly impressed by the way the bitch kept still, and Magda was impressed too.

Magda tried to imagine the Holy Spirit putting it in from behind and Mary on all fours like a bitch in her little hut made of straw. The little hut made of straw Magda could see very clearly, a hut not a stable. But the Holy Spirit putting it in from behind? No, that was just not possible. And even the other way round was absolutely impossible, because the Holy Spirit did not have a naked bum. And therefore there was no naked bum that could have moved up and down. That only left Joseph. Joseph gave Mary the baby Jesus. Mary, however, liked the story with the Holy Spirit, and Joseph probably too. It helped them to pretend they didn't do it, this thing that really didn't look nice. Surely the adults must know too how ugly it looks, how ugly it is to behave like pigs and dogs on heat and then to act as if nothing has happened. It was ugly and that was why the nuns said it was a sin and claimed that Mary didn't do it with Joseph like the pigs and dogs and believed in the story with the Holy Spirit. Well, that was fine with Magda. They could believe what they wanted. But Magda knew it wasn't true; she'd seen it, more than once. Perhaps the nuns had never seen it. It probably didn't really exist here behind these thick convent walls.

Magda pushes her left sleeve up, pinches herself on her lower arm, squeezing the skin between thumb and index finger. A sharp pain shoots up to her elbow and down to her wrist. She changes the position of the fingertips slightly, now digging the fingernails in as deep as possible, pulling and twisting the skin. She feels a twinge in her stomach, that's all. For a moment she wonders how much the pain could increase; she wants to see what happens when her whole body is filled with pain, what happens when she then keeps the pain inside herself. It might turn into something less awful, even something fascinating, which she then is able to observe in order to understand better what the suppressed squealing has to do with the ugly thing and why, despite the screaming and the ugliness, Mary, her mother and obviously many other women are doing it. Except, of course, the nuns.

The men do it because they have to, Egon Müller's son told her. 'It's the urge,' he explained. 'If you're a real man and not a sissy, well, you just have to put it somewhere.' And he showed her: he opened his trousers and took it out. At first Magda thought he wanted a piss, but then he said, 'I'll show you. Look at it.' He took the thing in his right hand; it was very small and disappeared inside his fist, a very black fist from the coal in the coal cellar. Egon Müller's son already worked in the coal cellar. And Magda saw the black fist, a glimmer of pale skin appearing here and there through the dirt. The hand started moving back and forth. They were standing in the corner behind the gate to the courtyard. At first she wanted to turn away and leave him standing there. But he suddenly grabbed her hard by the arm.

'Look!' he demanded, and she heard a groan escape his throat. He let go of her arm, took a step backwards, stood right beside her once more. He closed his eyes, leaning with his free hand against the wall in front of them, bending slightly forward, open-mouthed, his breathing becoming more laboured. Enthralled, Magda stared at his face. It had changed. He looked different now, still Egon Müller's son, but his face bore an expression of concentration, of preoccupation, which she hadn't seen before. A powerful feeling overwhelmed Magda: she ought to protect him, because he appeared somehow forlorn, he was so preoccupied. If in that moment Johnny had come with his gang, they could have just beaten him up. Egon Müller's son wouldn't have been aware of their coming, although he usually noticed everything. Magda had to be on her guard for him now, she was his protector. She liked his defencelessness. She held his fate in her hands. And with that thought she remembered Egon Müller's son's hand and that was the hand she was meant to look at. She tore her eyes away from his face – a pity really, because she enjoyed the moment of control. If Johnny had come, she could have warned him or not. Had she not warned him, they would have beaten him up. And had she warned him, she would have been his saviour. Never mind, she tore her eyes away from his face and fixed them on his dirty fist, on his dirty knuckles, up and down, up and down, at speed now, chop-chop. It took her a while to adjust to the acceleration, especially after the calm defencelessness of his face. But eventually she managed and then she realized that the thing had grown in his hand, popping out of the top of his fist, all rosy and clean, so beautifully clean, totally unlike the rest of Egon Müller's son. Again she heard him groan. Then he stopped. Opened his fist.

'Look at it!' he ordered her in deep, manly tones, also very different from his usual voice. 'Look at it. I told you

I'd show you, didn't I? Well, now you've got this thing and you just have to put it somewhere. That's how it works with us men. It's the urge – as a real man, you've simply got the urge.'

And his fist closed up again and continued its movement but at a slower pace.

'So, now you've got this thing and you've got to put it inside something, ideally inside a woman, between her legs – there it's soft and warm. But if that's not an option it also works like this.'

The movement quickened again and Magda observed every detail, her eyes glued to his fist. Egon Müller's son could hardly now talk, his voice breaking out of his throat spasmodically.

'Look . . . I'll show you . . . That's how it goes . . . I'll show you . . . I'll show you . . . I'll show you.'

He was groaning just like the man with her mother back at home. He began to irritate Magda because, truth be told, she'd seen it all before and this talk about I'll show you, I'll show you was nothing, just Egon Müller's son's way of boasting. This loser, he would never get out of his coal cellar. There were those who would get out of the coal cellar and those who would not, Magda knew that already. But then suddenly something spurted out into the air. It spurted, then it spurted out again. A white, milky liquid. Magda was mesmerized. Now, that was new. Egon Müller's son did indeed show her. She had to grant him that at least.

Magda now wonders where else to pinch herself in order to observe the pain, to understand what happens inside her body after the pain has entered it and is spreading. As if her body is a container made of glass and she, Magda, remains on the outside, observing her own body with the pain inside. A scientist dressed in a white coat in a laboratory. She'd once seen a photograph of a lady in a white coat in a laboratory holding a glass tube in her hand. When she's grown up, she wants to be just like this woman, wearing a long skirt and a white blouse with frills and a white coat over the top and her wavy hair held back in a bun. The photograph left a deep impression; the woman looked so clever and powerful and she was an observer all day long.

Magda had decided then and there she wanted to be just like that lady one day.

For the moment, however, she is still kneeling on the stone floor in front of the altar, in front of the wooden Virgin Mary. A bump in the stone is digging into her knee. Crying wouldn't help at all and wouldn't get her out of here either. Perhaps she should lie down and not get up again until someone picks her up. One of the big girls would certainly find her. And put her fully dressed under the cold water, where a disgusting smell of wet wool would soon rise up to her nostrils. And in the evening she'd sit in her wet clothes in the dining hall, shivering and with blue lips, as pale as a drowned corpse. Admittedly, she's never seen a drowned corpse, but she'd heard the other girls talk about it when Trude was shoved under the cold water because she didn't pull herself together and just cried and started to wet her bed and scratched her scalp until it bled. And then she even stopped eating. That's when the Mother Superior ordered a couple of the older girls to take Trude out into the yard and shower her with ice-cold water from the well. Cold water is good for you, wakes you up, and what doesn't kill you makes you stronger. Later on, when Magda saw the shivering Trude in the dining hall, she was overcome by a feeling of pity. They sat next to each other and, although they didn't touch, Magda felt the cold oozing out of Trude's body and enveloping her. Trude shivered, her teeth chattering and her hands pale and wrinkly. She stared at the crust of dry bread on her plate. The other girls were given hot soup with their bread. But not Trude, who needed to learn to eat up her crust again first. Magda kept her eyes fixed on her own plate, drinking her soup – hot water with disgusting little globules of fat. Out of the corner of her eye she watched Trude's fingers trying to catch hold of the bread. But Trude was shivering so violently that it fell out of her hand. 'Like a drowned corpse, that's what she looks like,' Céline whispered on the other side of the long wooden table. 'She's basically dead, just a trembling, drowned body.' The girls opposite giggled and the Mother Superior at the head of the table lifted her head and shouted, 'Quiet!' and then the only sound was Trude's chattering teeth. Once again Magda saw the hand stretching out, attempting to grab the crust. That's when she felt pity. She pressed her thigh against Trude's leg underneath the table, lifted her head and gave the girl a quick smile and a bit of her own body heat. And Trude managed to eat her bread.

In the following days, however, Trude began to follow Magda around like a shadow. A stray dog with big lost eyes and dark shadows underneath. Magda didn't like that at all. It felt irritating, like having a parasite attached to you. Eventually she led Trude into the dimly lit choir and pushed her up against the wall in the corner and raised her knee quickly into Trude's emaciated stomach.

'Don't bug me, do you understand?' Magda demanded.

'But I thought we were friends,' whined Trude.

'Friends? With someone who smells as disgusting as you? You reek of piss.'

Magda held Trude by the collar now and wanted to teach her a lesson. 'What did I tell you?' The girl was trembling again. Magda looked around, her eyes searching the half-dark choir until they fell upon the choirmaster's desk, where sheet music was piled up neatly, the choirmaster being a very neat man and keen on discipline and order. And Magda lifted Trude by the collar and pushed her against the desk, and she fell and took everything down with her. All the loose sheets of paper flew and fluttered and fell in a pleasantly spread-out way on the dirty wooden floorboards.

Magda had no choice. She did not want to be seen with Trude. She wasn't like Trude. She was no weak, needy parasite clinging to others, sucking their blood, only to get crushed at the end.

Of course Trude died, of consumption, three months later. Mass was said and one or two of the girls were probably a bit upset and embarrassed, because everyone had knocked Trude about, had kicked her every now and again, and perhaps it was this very kick that was too much. Or perhaps it wasn't this kick but that kick. Whatever. She could have defended herself and not just gazed with her large blue eyes, those inhuman eyes.

Not long after Trude had gone, the big girls found someone else who irritated them. Lotte. Magda hadn't noticed her, and although she was taller and older than Trude, she did indeed resemble her. Lotte had eventually caught the big girls' attention because she stayed far too long in that reeking cold shack where no one spent more time than necessary – except Lotte. The girls hammered on the door and shouted, 'Open up!' and had already pushed on the door before Lotte had time to hide the picture in the little secret bag that she carried around her neck underneath her dress. The girls grabbed the picture out of her hands. It showed a soldier. And they ripped the bag from Lotte's neck leaving a red mark. They found two letters from a man and Lotte's half-written reply. They cheered and shouted, 'Darling, sweetheart, my soul, my inner self is longing for you, you, my flower, my beautiful pink rosebud. When can I hold you, when can I see you opening?' They cheered and shouted and ran with the letter to the Mother Superior, who was shocked and fetched the cane and stayed a long time with Lotte behind closed doors.

'The Devil must be exorcized. Such disgusting indecency in God's house!' screamed the Mother Superior.

Then the girls outside the door heard only the hissing of the cane through the air and its slapping on naked skin. A large group of them waited eagerly outside, the oldest ones at the front with their ears pressed against the thick oak door.

'The Devil is deep inside you. How did he get in there? Through your openings, of course. We women have far too many openings, through which he crawls inside. Yes, and he lights a fire for us down there. You despicable brat, I will drive the Devil out of you. I won't have him here in my house.'

And then again a hissing followed by a smacking sound came reverberating through the air, through the thick oak door. Even right at the back Magda could hear it. The girls listened attentively to the performance, a staged exorcizing of the Devil, keenly awaiting Lotte's scream. But no scream came. The Devil sat deep inside her, had seized control of her, had perhaps already become one with her.

When suddenly the door opened, everybody jumped aside, surprised – no one had expected it. The Mother Superior appeared, her face dripping with sweat, the sleeves of her habit pushed up.

'Edith, Laurence, put her under cold water.'

Edith and Laurence scurried obediently past the Mother Superior and returned quickly with Lotte between them. Her dress was ripped at the back, a gaping tear from top to bottom revealing bleeding skin that had drenched the material red. Arms folded in front of her chest, Lotte tried to prevent her dress from slipping down.

The girls formed a double-line, gazing at this creature possessed by the Devil. The creature only vaguely resembled the Lotte they knew – truly she deserved her fate. To open a bud, how disgusting. Instinctively, though, the girls knew the show hadn't finished, there was more in the offing. Then it happened. The possessed creature stopped in her tracks, stood up straight, freed herself swiftly from the arms that were holding her, Edith's and Laurence's arms, and took a single giant leap towards the Mother Superior. For a moment time stood still, before the Devil spat right in the Mother Superior's face, then turned around and walked with head held high through the double-line formation, a victorious gleam in her eyes.

Lotte did appear at supper. Dark shadows were visible under her eyes. She didn't cry, her teeth didn't chatter, even though she was completely soaked and her back must have hurt. The tear in her dress was mended. She'd had to do it herself – badly, mind, a real shabby job, everyone could see that. She sat with her back straight and as she ate her crust of bread a smile flickered across her face. The next day she was dead. She had hanged herself from a beam in the dormitory in the middle of the night, had torn sheets and dresses. No one had heard her. Some had probably thought it was a dream. But the next morning there she was, hanging stark naked in the middle of the dormitory while the makeshift rope swung back and forth. The girls lay silently in their beds. Until Laurence suddenly shouted, 'Disgraceful! How dare she! What an awful sight. The poor little ones.' And then everybody shouted, 'Yes, the poor little ones. Avert your eyes, avert your eyes. What an awful, horrible sight!'

Laurence and Edith jumped out of bed, crossed themselves and gasped out a quick prayer. One got up on a chair, while the other held the legs of the corpse. They untied it and it fell onto the floor with a crash, and the little ones started to cry and the big ones took the little ones in their arms. 'Oh, you poor darlings, what an awful sight for little angels to behold.' The Mother Superior arrived. Perceiving the bedlam, she ordered an early morning Mass to cleanse the innocent souls.

Magda is now down on her knees, praying with all her heart to be protected from parasites and not to be led into the temptation to get mixed up with possessed soulless creatures. She does not want to die like them, squashed into oblivion. She would prefer to die like Mary, ascending into the heavens.

'Holy Mary, I beg you, give me faith and the will to be a virgin like you are.'

She throws herself down in front of the wooden statue and remains there for a long time, flat on her stomach, with her arms and legs spread out like a star.

THE MOTHER AND
THE COMMISSAR

My daughter had always wanted to be something special.
When she first met that Herr Doktor Goebbels I told her
straight away she should keep her hands off him. I was
dead set against her getting involved with someone in poli-
tics. I always kept clear of it myself. But my Magda was pig-
headed, wasn't she? You're doing all right now, I told her,
you've got your own apartment, ever so posh, and all kitted
out with fancy things. For her everything had to be the best,
it had to look the part, that's what my daughter felt was
important. Always behaving like she was an angel, she was,
a woman of the world, aloof. But in truth she was no better
than the rest of us. I never had it easy with that girl, not
from day one. I swear, there wasn't a single thing about her
that was easy. At the time I was in service in Bülowstrasse
and young Herr Ritschel soon took a shine to me. He was
really smart, that one. But when he asked for my hand in
marriage, his father, old Herr Ritschel, wasn't having any
of it. In old Ritschel's eyes I was a mere maidservant, so
he packed his son off to Belgium – he was a trained engi-
neer, after all – and then he came to me, the father I mean,

and begged me not to say a word about who the child's father was. And provided I kept my mouth shut he'd give me money each month. Well, of course I kept my mouth shut. I didn't want to end up with my little one in the gutter. I brought her into the world all alone on the eleventh of the eleventh in the year one, and called her Johanna Maria Magdalena. She screamed from the very first day. I was dead embarrassed. You see, all of the neighbours thought there was no husband.

(The old woman adjusts the bag on her lap.)

But I'll tell you one thing, I bet they were all pretty surprised when he turned up one day and married me. It wasn't a big wedding – his father had just recently passed away – but from that day onwards I had a man in the house. And a marvellous one at that, with a fur-trimmed coat if you please! He continued to work in Belgium, but he always came back to visit us. He assumed he'd be returning to Berlin and so it wasn't worth our while moving there.

(She sniffles.)

Oh, the things you play along with, eh?

(She looks up misty-eyed at the commissar.)

I'm afraid to say my marriage to Herr Ritschel didn't last very long. After that the child and I were alone once more. He'd send money from time to time, but it wasn't anything regular, like. And then one day there he is at my front door again. He wants to send the girl to a decent school, that's his duty as a father, he says. I invited him in and made him a nice cup of coffee, with real coffee beans, you know, that's what I had in those days, and when we were sitting opposite each other at the table, I got the feeling he wanted to have his way with me again. But I said to him I wasn't having a fling with him now, on account of I was being courted by someone else. And I was against cheating on principle. Well, then he backed down and acted like he wanted nothing from me at all. He talked about the convent where he intended to send our little madam, where she'd learn to be a proper lady. At first I didn't want to give the child away just like that, but this convent school in Belgium, situated close to where he worked, sounded good. Best of all it would mean that the girl wouldn't be hanging around the streets any more. I mean, I had things to do and I couldn't always keep an eye on her. And I was desperate for her to have a better life than me, her own mother. So we agreed that in a few days' time I'd put the girl on the train to Cologne, and he'd be there already as he had some business to attend to. From there they'd travel together to Belgium. On the day I packed her sandwiches and fruit and milk, and hung a sign around her neck so that everybody could see who this cheeky monkey was, where she'd come from and where she was going. When we got to the station I handed her over to the guard. And do you know what that little monkey did during the journey? She threw the bottle out of the window with all that lovely milk in it. She said a big girl like her didn't need milk any more. Told me the story herself years later, she did. Well, I never saw her for two years afterwards. Herr Ritschel didn't even give me the name of the convent. I begged him and pleaded with him – but it was no use. During that time Herr Friedländer, the shopkeeper, came into my life. I've never had anything against Jews, you see. Herr Friedländer was a Jew. I fell head over heels in love. I was totally gone on him, like I was a young girl again. Then suddenly he gets this idea into his head that we should fetch the girl from the convent. A child belongs in a family, he said, a proper family. He proposed to me and said he wanted to adopt the girl and give her his name. At first I was uneasy about the whole thing. I mean, what would Ritschel, her real father, say? I tried to warn Herr Friedländer that he shouldn't mess with Ritschel. After all, he was a dyed-in-the-wool Catholic and had it in for the Jews on account of Jesus and because they controlled all the banks and screwed businessmen for every last penny. But, to cut a long story short, I finally saw Herr Friedländer's point and I sent a telegram to Belgium, and then, all of a sudden, Herr Ritschel gave me the address. I left straight away. I mean, I was desperate to see my little darling again. And, good God! The poor little creature! It was horrific in that convent. Freezing cold everywhere, draughty, and all the girls sleeping in the same dormitory. Well, I took her out there and then, didn't I? The poor thing was as thin as a rake. Herr Friedländer arrived after me, and together we found another convent for Magda, not as strict, in Vilvoorde. Ritschel insisted that the girl had to stay in Belgium, didn't he? In Vilvoorde the dormitory was divided up into cubicles which you could close off with a curtain. Each girl had a bed in her own little corner, a chair and a cabinet for her clothes. At night-time a nun would go up and down the dormitory saying the Divine Office and the Rosary. The daily routine was still pretty strict, mind you. The girls had to get up at the crack of dawn and go to early Mass in the church – on an empty stomach, if you please! Once, my Magda passed out, and after that she was given special permission to eat a piece of chocolate before Mass – chocolate that I'd brought her when I visited. I was a real nervous wreck back then. And nothing could have made me leave Belgium. We were lucky that Herr Friedländer had some business in Belgium, and when our circumstances improved we were able to rent a pretty little house in Hortensienallee, and then Magda went to a day school nearby and I had a little vegetable garden. It took me a while to see that Herr Friedländer only had eyes for Magda. Guarded her like gold, he did. If I'm being honest I think he only married me on account of my daughter. I don't want you getting the idea that he was some kind of lecher. No, no, I wouldn't have got involved with a lecher who's only after young girls. He was no lecher, it was all very proper how he behaved, it was just that he had this little notion in his head. He had a thing about daughters, you see. He'd always wanted a daughter, and being the father of a girl made him feel marvellous. I'm sure in his head he thought he was some kind of hero. As I say, he guarded Magda like gold. Spoilt her rotten, didn't he? And made her think she was somebody. So then in Berlin – we had to leave Belgium, you see, when the war started – in Berlin he immediately enrols her in the secondary school in Keithstrasse, so she won't miss any school. My God, I made quite a fuss, I tell you. I mean, the girl couldn't even speak proper German. I really did try my best after we'd got her back to a decent home in Brussels. But it was those awful years in the convent, when Herr Ritschel refused to tell me where he'd sent her. She only spoke French there, you see, so she forgot her mother tongue completely. If it had been up to me, the first thing I'd have done was to teach her proper German again. But spoilt rotten that girl was, all hoity-toity; she thought she was better than the rest of us and was above it all. It would've done her the world of good to go to work when we arrived back in Berlin. I'd actually found her a place in a factory, you know, even though those were hard times. I knew what was good for my daughter. Needed to get to know her place, she did, learn how to conform a little. I wanted her to have to struggle, to grin and bear it, so she'd get an idea of how the world really works. Get her down from that pedestal of hers where she stood. I'd have loved to wipe that smug look off her stuck-up face. She'd look at me silently, she would, judging me. I ought to have followed my instincts and stuck her in that factory, that would've got rid of those silent stares pretty sharpish. No more skulking in the corner and gawping at people, no, she wouldn't have been able to carry on like that in the factory.

(The woman sniffles again.)

But Herr Friedländer decided differently. I'd already started making her sandwiches for the factory when he suddenly flies into a rage, first thing in the morning, shouting his head off all over the place. That man had really forgotten his manners. It sorely dented his pride when us Germans were packed onto a train and bundled out of Belgium just like that. And then he couldn't get at his money, because it was in the bank in Brussels and they'd closed all the accounts. So there he was, screaming his head off early in the morning, asking me what on earth I thought I was doing putting his daughter in the factory. I'd been doing it all on the sly, he said. 'Stupid woman!' he screamed at me, purple in the face. 'You stupid woman! I'm not going to let you mess up my daughter.' I sat on the bed and all I could do was howl. So humiliating. I mean, we lived like bloody rats in that place, and we had to share a room with another family – all that separated the two halves of the room was a blanket – and there was us living in one of the poshest parts of Brussels just before. I'll have you know I'm a respectable woman and there he was tearing strips off me. What was I to do? Shriek back at him like I was some old fish wife? The neighbours would've loved that. No, I kept calm, stayed as quiet as a mouse, and just let him scream the place down – that scrawny little Jew who I'd once smiled at in a moment of weakness. God, you pay for your mistakes in life, don't you? What was I to do? I'd love you to tell me. All those years ago! I mean, I was still a young girl when all of a sudden there he is standing in the doorway, giving me the eye and going on about roses and love, and saying he's yearning for me. I ask you, what young woman could resist that for long? Especially seeing as I was lonely and keen on getting myself a decent husband. And now this was payback time. The neighbour, fat old Frau Kunze – well, I bet she was having a good old giggle listening to him shouting. She was just waiting for me to join in the slanging match, but I've got my pride. I just wept quietly. Didn't say a word, not even when he grabbed poor Magda's thin little wrist and dragged her along behind him. Dragged her the whole way to school, he did. I said nothing. Afterwards I bumped into Frau Kunze on the landing, gave her a smile and said, 'Good morning,' acted like nothing had happened. 'Nothing to do with me, that screaming. Must have been someone else being yelled at, God knows who.' That's how I dealt with it anyhow. He conned me out of love and happiness. Jewish con-merchant. But I've paid for my mistakes, that's for sure. And I've taken my punishment on the chin.

(The commissar interrupts the woman, leans over the desk towards her, says something unintelligible, then leans back and waits, keeping his eyes fixed on her.)

You want me to get back to talking about my daughter. All right, then. My daughter. As was blindingly obvious, or let's say as was blindingly obvious to me, matters only got worse with the girl. She started ignoring me. She's out the door at the crack of dawn – soon after that we got our own small flat again; that was my doing by the way, I found it for us – so that Magda, she's out the door at the crack of dawn and then you didn't see her again for the rest of the day. She started gadding about. I told Friedländer that's what she was doing, but he just shook his head, didn't he? She's not gadding about, he said, she's got a friend and they do their schoolwork together. So then she'd come home, sit at the table and gobble down her soup with her head stuck in a book. Wouldn't say a word to her mother. And believe me, I tried to talk to her. At the beginning, anyhow. At some point, of course, the whole thing just got too stupid. I wasn't going to let myself be treated like I was invisible, screamed at by one of them and treated like I was invisible by the other. Finally, she didn't even want my soup. 'I've already eaten,' she'd say, and shut herself in her room. So

I started spying on her, didn't I? She was my daughter after all, and I needed to know if she was going off the rails. But my daughter was always able to look after herself. When I found out what she was getting up to, I knew in a flash that all my fussing was a waste of time. I felt like a right fool. She'd only gone and found herself another family, something a bit better, seeing as ours wasn't in such great shape. And with this new lot she came and went as she pleased, and I soon realized what it was about them she was so taken with. I was dumbstruck. So much for the schoolwork! She'd been making eyes at this lad, hadn't she? And old Friedländer was protecting her. They were Jews as well, the Arlosoroffs. So finally I lost my rag with him, I snapped and booted him out. At that moment I didn't give a fig. About the neighbours or nothing. That man, that blighter had destroyed my life, ruined it. When I met him I was still young and beautiful, avenues were open to me, I had possibilities, the world was my oyster. He seduced me – put a spell on me, he did. He definitely put a spell on me; nobody could've stuck with him for that long otherwise. You know, I swear there must've been some little thing he did which totally switched off my common sense, I'm sure of it. It was like waking up out of a long sleep – do you know what I mean? – and when I finally woke up and was able to see what had happened to me, what he'd done to me, I was old. I looked in the mirror and saw this fat old woman dressed in rags. What more could I expect to get out of life? And as far as my daughter was concerned I didn't exist any more. Know what I did then? I just hid myself away. After all, I knew that no one cared two hoots whether I stayed in bed or not. I was ill, you see, sick at heart, and no one was there to look after me. I saw her, my daughter, in the gateway with that good-for-nothing Jew . . .

(The woman sits up in the chair, her hands clutch the bag on her lap and she curls her lip angrily.)

Let's just forget it, shall we?

(It is late now. A dim evening light is just visible through the dirty window; in half an hour it will be dark. The commissar feels in his trouser pocket, removes a packet of cigarettes, taps one out on the table and lights it. His first cigarette of the day. He only smokes in the evenings. He leans back in his chair and blows smoke rings in the air. For a brief moment he switches off from listening. For some time he's had his doubts about whether there's any point to this whole process. Especially with this woman. No one has talked for as long as she has. Most of them say pretty quickly that they knew nothing, and that their sons, daughters, husbands, wives, nieces, brothers-in-law, and whoever else have always been decent people and there must be some mistake – yes, there definitely must be some mistake. What other explanation can there be? And then the commissar forces these people to look at pictures, the heaps of bones and living skeletons. They stare at them; maybe they stare straight through the photographs. There was only one woman who had a fit of hysteria, saying it wasn't true. The Yanks, the world, the enemy had made it all up, it was all trick photography. And she'd brought other photographs out of her bag, showing the bodies of muscular men and women in part shade. 'That's what the Nazis were all about,' she'd said, 'purity, beauty and unity. Look, take a look at these pictures. We're going to build a new German empire.'

The old woman is the first one who has really talked. But the commissar is not wholly sure what she has been saying. Perhaps someone can analyse it later and make use of it. After all, her daughter was the wife of one of the most powerful Nazis; she was a true fanatic, a child murderer.

He forces himself to concentrate again on the woman's monologue.)

One of the loveliest moments of my life was when Magda came to me and said she wanted to train for domestic service rather than continue studying. I'd had my doubts, you see, that she'd ever be a respectable person, what with her head having been turned, twisted really, round and round and round like in a vice, so that it was perched there on her long thin neck, looking down on everybody, especially her own flesh and blood, her own mother. With those cold . . . those ice-cold eyes. But he put her back on the straight and narrow, didn't he? He, who'd never let us down, because . . .

(She suddenly lowers her voice.)

He'd always loved me in fact – yes, he had. With his help she'd got back on the straight and narrow.

(The woman pauses abruptly and looks down at her hands, which are clutching the bag. She bites the inside of her lip.)

I mean, I find it very hard to ask people for help.

(Another pause. She slowly raises her head and looks at the commissar.)

But back then I did ask him for help. I mean, what does

pride count for when it's your own child? Only a mother can have such feelings, you know. Only a mother. There are times you'd do anything for your own child. And that was such a time. I said to myself, Auguste, I said, you just swallow your pride and go and see him. So I made myself all smart, I did, new suit, and I didn't even send a telegram to warn him, I just got on the train and went straight there. He was in Cologne now, you see, he'd become established there again. Of course, I was nice and discreet. At the reception I said I was the gentleman's cousin, just passing through, and was it possible to speak to him briefly. Well, I imagine he got a bit of a surprise. I don't think he recognized me at first. Then he just sat there, speechless, behind his desk. I sat down on the chair all calm like, waited a moment until he got a proper look at me. Of course my heart was pounding, but I didn't want to let on. I just kept on telling myself that I was doing it for my daughter. So finally I said, 'We've got to talk about Magda.' All very calm. You'd have been proud of me, Herr Commissar. A real woman of the world. He then took me out to lunch. And we talked about Magda. I told him about the good-for-nothing Jew she was hanging around with and that I'd seen them in the gateway and was that what he wished for his daughter. Was that what he'd given his money for all these years, and if he didn't watch it he'd soon be shelling out for a little bastard and all. Because I couldn't, could I? Well, that sent a shiver down his spine, let me tell you. And he said he'd sort it out. He's a good, upright man; would you mind noting that in your files? In case he gets accused of anything. He kept to his word. Took Magda under his wing, introduced her into society, gave her a taste for a certain type of life. Showed her how easy life was if you're a member of the right class. You might say I helped my daughter have everything that had been closed off to me, unfortunately. Anyway, as I was saying, the nicest day, or at least one of them, was when she comes home and tells me she wants to train for domestic service. At last we'd left all that Jewish intellectual stuff behind us. I'd been in a cold sweat, I had. Imagined she'd come and say she wanted to study. Another few years idled away. I mean, in those days everything seemed suddenly possible for women. And then what? What would happen after? No one would've wanted her then. Me and her father, him shelling out for her for the rest of our lives. I wanted something respectable for my daughter. But then the training for domestic service never got off the ground. That led to a pretty ugly scene between Magda and me. I was supposed to have applied to the training school on her behalf because she was only eighteen, still under age. But I'd got the date wrong in my head. Such mistakes happen, don't they? But Magda had no patience with little human errors. She was really shirty about it. Only years later she admitted there'd been no reason for her behaving like that. Absolutely no reason at all. Because not long after, she met that very respectable Herr Direktor Quandt on the train. He was twenty years older than her, but she was completely smitten. I had my misgivings right from the start, and I told my daughter so. Herr Direktor Quandt was a widower and had a son who was almost as old as Magda. I really didn't think that it was going to end well. But Magda was impressed by his position, his wealth, his influence. So then the two of them go and get married. And not long after, Harald was born, a few days after Magda's twentieth birthday. At that point the troubles between my daughter and Herr Direktor Quandt had already started. Although he took her to Paris and Munich and God knows where else, he was always falling asleep in the theatre, and once even halfway through a bowl of soup when they were having dinner. Well, of course my daughter wasn't going to put up with that sort of behaviour. Her admirers had to dance attendance on her, didn't they? And if they didn't dance to her tune straight away, my daughter didn't show much forgiveness. Forgiveness was not in her reach. So one day there she was at my door again with little Harald. Herr Direktor Quandt proved to be very easy-going over the divorce and settlement. I suspect part of him was quite relieved to be rid of my daughter. And maybe he felt a little bit guilty too. I mean, he wasn't able to offer her everything she was after. On the other hand, my daughter surely had too high standards. I don't know, it just often seemed that way, especially in her relations with men. That was even the case with Herr Doktor Goebbels – although I'm really not looking to defend him now – and all his women troubles. Him too, somehow she managed to put him under so much pressure that he went off looking elsewhere. Everyone knew. That's what men are like. If you put them under too much pressure they fly off into another nest where it's warmer. My daughter simply had some funny ideas about life and strange expectations, especially with men. That's why no one stuck with her for long. Before she met Herr Doktor Goebbels she'd had one or two lovers.

She didn't introduce them to me. But you pick up the odd thing, don't you? And she'd started mingling with the smart set, on account of her apartment. She was able to rent it with the money she'd got from the settlement. All of a sudden she was someone. She'd be up all night sometimes. And every week she'd have a couple of new dresses made, if you please. I heard it all from Frau Feld, my dear old dressmaker, who I'd go to see maybe once a month to have the odd hem taken up or button sewn on, you know, nothing grand – I mean, I've always been a thrifty woman – and then Frau Feld would tell me all the details. 'Oh yes, your daughter, two new silk dresses, last week a suit with mink, and for next week she's got a blue tulle evening dress.' Occasionally I'd walk past her apartment on the way to the market. The curtains were always drawn until late in the afternoon. Sometimes I bumped into her maid at the market and I'd often hear how the mistress had a headache. That was just one of her maids. The next one was even more of a gossip. Oh, the mistress was out almost every night, and sometimes she'd bring a gentleman back with her. That maid didn't last long either. A right unpredictable one, my daughter. If someone complained, they were out on their ear. And she didn't always pay the maids what they were owed. Back then the world was in a real state. Only my Magda saw it differently. She just seemed to dance, make merry and have endless fun. And then one day she's suddenly sitting there howling at my kitchen table. Her life was so boring, she said, she felt like she was dead inside. Well, you could have knocked me down with a feather! I hadn't a clue what to say to her. Pretty sharpish I suspected there must be a man behind it. But Magda just shook her head, still sobbing. No, and I shouldn't talk such nonsense, it's not always to do with men. Men would queue up to be with her and she could choose a new one for herself every day. But in the end it's always the same. She was terrified by the idea that her life might go on like that for ever. Well, of course I felt sorry for her, and I gave her the advice. She should get married again, have children, they'd fill her empty life. She didn't want any more children, she said, she wanted to achieve something special. Yes, those were her very words. She didn't want children, she wanted to achieve something special, only she didn't know what. Well, I blame old Friedländer for all that. Yes, I do. Her head just got turned and never went back to where it should have been. I sat down next to her and listened to her going on about achieving something special, about how she'd been chosen for something, had a calling, like a man. Only she didn't know what. She had to make something of her life, she said. There was so much fire in her belly, but as she didn't know what to do with it, it was just going to die. She was wasting away, she said. I got a real fright, I tell you. Thought, perhaps my daughter is ill, sick in the head. I tried to talk to her. We women, I said, we are there to give birth to children and bring them up. If she had a few more children, I said, her life wouldn't seem so bleak any more. And then, just as suddenly as she'd turned up with her eyes full of tears, she stopped weeping. Just like that. All at once she lifts up her head. I'm still in the middle of talking to her, doing my best to comfort her, and she lifts up her head. The tears have already vanished, not the slightest trace of them on her cheeks; she looks at me with her icy gaze – you can't work out what's going on behind those eyes – and says, 'Mother, that's enough.' She gets up and a few seconds later I can hear the door to my apartment closing behind her. I can hear her steps in the landing. Like rifle shots. Rat-a-tat-tat. Mechanical. I run to the window and through the net curtain I see her go out of the gate and on to the street. Hat on, coat done up, handbag jammed under her arm, off she goes with her head held high. Well, that's how she was. There was a part of her that was tough as nails.

(The woman leans forward, places her bag beside her on the floor, sits back, leans forward again and puts her head in her hands. She is sniffling audibly. She sits up straight once more. Her face is red and tears are rolling down her cheeks.)

You've got to understand that it wasn't always easy with Magda. I mean, there I am, watching her strut off, all rat-a-tat-tat with those steps that sounded like hammer blows and her head in the air, and the next thing I know she's at my front door again, and now she's all involved with that new party, isn't she? All gleaming eyes and red cheeks, hands me a leaflet and says that the Führer's coming to Berlin tomorrow, he's giving a speech and I've absolutely got to be there. She'd joined the party now, they needed women, she was head of the local women's group. The National Socialists were a young party, she said, and their leader was a man with a vision for the future. They needed good women like her, she said.

THE CALLING

There He stands before Magda, a little man on a podium who has assumed the stature of a giant using nothing but simple words and a strident voice. She stands right at the back in the smoky hall. He stands at the other end, in front of the people, and He looks straight at her. Magda goes home and reads His books and understands that here is a man who took one look at history and put the stark facts into perspective. This man believes in meaning, this man delivers meaning, this man is meaning. He is mind without body and Magda is inspired; the spirit has entered her, the Holy Spirit has come to her and taken her, planting a seed in her as he did with the Virgin Mary.

She joins the local women's association in her borough. An old hall with stucco moulding and bad lighting and a rickety black grand piano pushed into the corner. The dark red flowery wallpaper has faded into a musty pink. Magda notices immediately that she is the most elegant person in the room; the others are simple women with flat shoes and brown woollen cardigans. Many lost sons or husbands in the war. They talk about Him and how He gives them hope, how He will provide work and give everyone back their dignity. The mood is depressed and weighs heavy on Magda's shoulders, but she comes back the next time, keeps to herself, listens to the talking and complaining of the women. They cannot organize themselves, that is obvious; they are getting bogged down in words. The following week Magda proposes the opening of a soup kitchen, under the name of His party. It would be a good way for His name and the name of His party to be spread among the poor and the needy. And besides, hot soup is always welcome. The women are sceptical – the tall blonde one in the mink stole and high heels is proposing a soup kitchen? But Magda cannot be dissuaded: she divides up the women for cooking duties. The following day the women turn up with big pots of soup and Magda positions herself behind a table outside by the entrance to the hall, holding a ladle in her hand. She serves with a smile. More soup is being cooked and Magda's smile brightens. Men queue up and when the soup is finished they queue up to catch a smile from the beautiful blonde in her high-heeled shoes with the mink around her shoulders. That mink stole soon becomes her trademark, the ice-blonde one with the stole, whose smile melts hunger and poverty into nothingness. Magda has flyers printed and asks Frau Lehmann's boys to distribute them in town. Even more soup is being cooked and Magda holds everybody's gaze when she ladles it out. People perceive her as generous, a patroness, a benefactress, while she pretends to herself that she is a priestess in flowing robes, a priestess who bestows her blessings upon the common people.

Then one day the masses suddenly fall silent, stepping aside as if under orders, opening up a pathway down the middle. Once again Magda has just lifted her head with a red smile on her lips and the full ladle in her hand. A car approaches and stops in front of the table. The door opens and He steps out, followed by Joseph. A murmur goes through the crowd and whispering sighs escape the mouths of the women, who suddenly all hide behind her. Only Magda does not murmur as her eyes rest on Him. A little round man, with a ridiculously tiny moustache no wider than his nose, a thin wisp of hair combed backwards across a bald patch – an inconspicuous, ugly little man dressed in a far too big beige raincoat tightened around his belly like a monk's habit, with thin old man's legs in chequered socks sticking out of knickerbockers. Her eyes rest on His eyes, watery blue like hers, as He walks towards her, approaching the table. And she lowers the ladle into the pot and steps from behind the table. She bows her head. She curtsies. He lifts His hand and lays it upon her head. 'My child, do get up. It is I who should lower himself in front of you.' And His hand rises from her head and places itself underneath her chin and her chin rests in His palm and He lifts her head. And she knows she has received benediction and she straightens herself and she looks over His shoulder and sees Joseph.

The following day Magda receives a personal letter from Joseph, cordially inviting her to accept an invitation to an official dinner with Him. Frau Feld will make her a pearl-grey evening dress with sequins and a narrow waist and a little train in less than forty-eight hours. That evening she laughs and drinks and eats, and Joseph's eyes rest on her lips, her breasts. They are only a small party, ten people, three women and seven men – and Him, presiding at the head of the table. He does not drink alcohol and has brought His own soup, which He pours from a metal container into His bowl.

'My child, eat. I enjoy watching you.'

He leans forward ever so slightly towards her. When He talks normally, rather than screaming down from a podium, He keeps His voice low, slightly muffled and tentative, as if it wasn't pumped up completely. It conveys a kind of parental solicitude, the attitude of one who enjoys watching his little darlings play.

'Don't you ever drink?' she asks.

'My stomach is very sensitive, my child. I have to look after myself.'

He stops, leans back in His chair and smiles at her, this blonde beauty, with adoring eyes.

'But you, my child, you should have fun. You are a woman with real strength, I can feel that.'

Magda smokes and drinks and talks and on the dance floor she spins around in Joseph's arms, even though Joseph is not a good dancer. She doesn't mind, as she dances under His gaze, sensing Him watching over Joseph and her as if protecting them. In His eyes they are dancing a beautiful dance; in His eyes they are a beautiful, perfect couple. And soon she and Joseph are overcome by the sensation that they are two children playing under the watchful, perceptive eyes of a father, knowing that as long as they keep on playing they will receive this calming, parental acknowledgement. Also later on, when she and Joseph can't wait to get to the bedroom and instead do it on the Persian carpet, next to the black pianoforte, where he whispers in her ear something like, 'You are my sweet flower. I have picked you. Let me feast on your sweet honey,' she hears the words and feels his hands and sees herself with Joseph through His eyes. She knows He is watching although He isn't physically present and it is a comforting feeling to perform under His care the most human act, because it is He who gives it meaning and His blessing through His own purity.

She offers her body to Joseph and her spirit to Him, and she feels completeness and belonging. She gives birth to their first child, then the second and third. Joseph is disappointed in her, because they are only girls and next time he expects a boy. But He is totally besotted with the three little blondes, miniature versions of their mother. He already sees the vast Russian land populated by blonde, blue-eyed angels. If He'd been a man like any other He would have taken Magda himself, lain down beside her. But earthly flesh isn't His calling; He knows only the spirit. Flesh repulses Him, His own and that of others. It took Him years of introspection until He understood that His fear of flesh was a sign of His non-earthly, non-human being. It is a gift, a responsibility, and it is His duty to use it for the good of mankind.

'My child, please, pull yourself together.'

He sits opposite Magda in a big armchair, relaxed it seems, both arms on the armrests, legs crossed. She is perched on a stool.

'I can't take any more. I will leave Joseph.'

'You can take much more. You and I, we are made from the same mould. I understand you, my child, and you know that. You can take much more, I am sure of that.'

'He humiliates me, goes with other women, even brings them home. I am no longer the mistress of my own house.'

'Of course you are the mistress. He brings them—'

'Little provincial actresses, singers, dancers . . . coquettes really, that's what he brings home, enjoying—'

'He brings them home like a cat brings home a mouse to play with in front of its owner, letting it run back and forth between its paws for a while before the kill. He wants your approval, that's all.'

'When a cat catches a mouse, it does what it is born to do. When Joseph brings home these women . . . before my very eyes, these little coquettes—'

'My child, you have to understand, what he does he can only do in front of you, because you are his true mistress. The urges he satisfies with these girls are unworthy of you. Joseph knows that. He is only human and weak; he is not like you and I. Every now and then we might feel impulses, but we don't have to satisfy them. The pleasures of the flesh are hollow and fleeting. My dearest, please don't despair. I need you.'

He leans forward, takes her hands.

'I need you and the German people need you too. You are their icon. German women believe in you. Because you stand beside your man, they can stand beside their men.'

'But it's just a big lie. Where is it all going to end?'

He lets go of her hands abruptly, leans back again.

'Where it will all end? That's what you are asking me, my child, my dearest, my most loyal friend – you, whom I could rely upon from the first moment? You ask me where will it all end? In the creation of a new nation, the resurrection of the Aryan race – a body nearly bled to death is stirring again. We are removing the leeches and with each one we remove we are regaining strength, and slowly but surely we are returning to our former might and reclaiming the land that is ours by right, spreading out and giving back hope to all mankind.'

Magda is now looking at Him with dry eyes. There is this question that buzzes around in her head. Always this question that, if asked, He might regard as treason.

'We are not creating anything with this war. We don't give hope. We destroy, we annihilate.'

For a moment He looks at her silently. She is waiting for her punishment because she dared to venture too far. He doesn't like to see His actions questioned. She is bracing herself for the inevitable storm. She is longing for this storm to arrive, hoping that she will be tossed aside by it, overwhelmed, so that she no longer needs to think for herself and can thus be released from all responsibility. Every bit of doubt will be swept away; anxiety will no longer grab hold of her, crush her heart, only to leave it behind – again and again – as a raw, open wound. Soon she will be soothed by delirious nothingness.

'Photographs of mass human graves and mountains of human bones lie in Joseph's desk drawer.'

She is provoking Him, summoning the storm – may it break now.

An expression of grief flits across His face.

'My child, do you understand what you are doing here? Usually in a situation like this, I would now get up and walk away. I don't discuss these matters. Because most people can't even begin to understand. They don't understand that this is what they wanted and that's why it is happening. Those people – every member of the German nation, of the Aryan race – have worked towards this goal for generations, for centuries. The only thing I have done is to make flesh that which they have summoned in words, in thought. The human race wants these pictures. I show them what they want; I show them their will. But people don't want to see their own will. They want to hide it, keep it in the dark, as if we are all still living in the womb. I give the human race the opportunity to see. I stand guard while they finally leave their mother's womb.'

For a brief moment He stops, but then He continues: 'My dear, don't you ever speak of destruction. Because we don't destroy. We are in the midst of a magnificent, unique undertaking. We are inaugurating the next stage in the development of mankind. We are guiding people out of their caves, where they have lived until now, where the will has been allowed to rage blindly. We are leading them into the light. Now mankind has no choice but to see and accept. That is what these photographs are for. One day the human race will be grateful to us that we were strong enough to accomplish this task. And free mankind from the Jews, those smooth-talking storytellers, those liars with their myths of their unique god and his chosen people.'

He suddenly looks tired, slumps back into the chair. His right hand is shaking; dark shadows have appeared under the eyes; a single greasy hair lies stuck to the forehead. She slides down from her seat onto her knees in front of Him.

'My Führer, forgive me my doubts. Forgive me.'

'Go home and show compassion towards your husband. The task at hand is too much for him. Forgive Joseph his trespasses and live like a saint, because you are a saint.'

Magda is still kneeling in front of Him. He holds out His hand to help her up. She takes it and presses it against her forehead, then lets it glide down towards her lips, presses her lips first into His palm and then onto the back of His hand. Thus she would gladly remain for eternity, never wanting to lift her head again, never wanting to get up again. She belongs in this position; this position belongs to her; she was made flesh to be here, on her knees in front of Him, with her lips touching His hand. This is why she was born.

HELGA'S DIARIES

Dearest Gretchen,

I am in such a state. Something terrible has happened and I will never be able to make up for it. Never. Only to you can I confess how far I am from perfection, how corrupted by sin. I have sinned against my parents, the Führer, my beautiful Fatherland. I wish I could die. My hand is shaking, but I have to calm down because I want to tell you, my dear, beautiful, patient diary, what has happened.

I sat on the swing in the garden. Today was such a delightful spring day, not a single cloud in the sky; the birds were singing; the first couple of bees were buzzing; you could hear the gentle rustling of the leaves in the wind and the murmuring of the stream at the bottom of our garden. Two cabbage white butterflies danced in front of my eyes. My heart was as light as a feather. Suddenly I became aware of two soldiers. They are not supposed to be in our garden, as they are often rough, boorish lads who frighten me. Quickly and quietly, I slid down from the swing and hid behind a tree. It was not my intention to eavesdrop on them; I just didn't want them to see me. There I stood and only a few steps away from me were these two lads. I didn't breathe. I closed my eyes and pressed myself as closely as possible up against the trunk of the old horse chestnut. I heard the striking of a match and a moment later cigarette smoke blew in my direction. I couldn't tell if they had changed position but it felt to me as if the smoke had got stronger, as if they had come closer. Suddenly frightened, I opened my eyes wide, convinced I could already hear them breathing right next to me. Unable to move, I was glued to the tree trunk. I wouldn't be able to escape.

'Hitler is basically dead. He won't carry on much longer,' one of the voices said, before continuing: 'Reiner, listen, the war is over, everything lost. We should save our own skins, that's all we can do now.'

'Do you think so?' the other one asked. Timidly, quietly. 'That's treason, Otto. They can shoot us for that.'

'The officers are leaving first. It's all over.'

'Helga!' Mother's voice from the house stopped the conversation.

'Helga!' Again Mother's voice.

I just couldn't move. Hitler dead! The war lost! What were they talking about? A painful fear gripped my heart and pushed me in the direction of the house. Finally I was able to run, though the path from the swing to the house seemed endless. But eventually I reached the front porch. I didn't stop in the hallway, rushing immediately down the stairs into the kitchen, as it seemed to me that Mother's voice had come from there. And indeed, there were Mother and my dear siblings sitting together around the table, huddled close to the warm stove. And I just wasn't able to keep quiet and had to destroy this peaceful picture.

'We've lost the war. And Uncle Adolf is dead.'

An indescribable look of horror came over their faces. I noticed Mother's twitching left eye. The pain behind her forehead must have been unbearable. All of a sudden I felt someone grabbing my arm from behind. I was turned around and Father's horrified face appeared in front of me. He scolded me badly for lying. And from his raised hand I could tell that I had driven him to the brink of madness. My shame is huge. I've never seen my gentle father even hurt a fly before, let alone smacking us children. Mother, yes, from time to time, and also Bertha, but never Father.

Humans need hope and faith in order to live. Some are born with the ability to have faith, to have hope. They are the blessed ones, like the Führer, Father and Mother. Most people, however, are born without hope and faith, but they can learn it from a Führer. And then there are people like me. We have to struggle, to fight for our faith and hope. We have to be continuously aware of the enemy inside us. We are never allowed to let go.

IN THE BUNKER, 23 APRIL 1945

Dearest Gretchen,

I have shamefully neglected you for five days. Please don't be angry with me. My heart is kind and I mean no harm. There has been a lot of excitement. We have left Schwanenwerder and are now in the bunker of our Führer.

As a writer and a poetic spirit, I cannot close my eyes and shut out reality, which – my poor little Gretchen, you are the lucky one who hasn't got any eyes – looks grim. We all now hope for a quick end to the war. I sincerely believe that even Father and Uncle Adolf have tired of the war. The enthusiasm for it has gone. There is a depressed feeling here in the bunker, although everyone is very busy. Constant comings and goings, meetings behind closed doors, a lot of whispering. And sadly also a lot of drinking among the young lads. Uncle Adolf, who usually looks after the health of his soldiers and loved ones so well, doesn't seem to notice for once. Or he has decided to turn a blind eye. I don't like passing those drunken lads and I always keep my eyes chastely lowered. But otherwise I feel very secure here in the bunker. We all feel well protected. From above you can hear continuous bombardment. Last night, too. It must have been terrible up there. But we won't abandon the fight for our dear city, because if Berlin falls, the German Reich will fall. I am glad now that from an early age Father told me stories about old battles. Thus I know that war belongs to mankind like the roots to a tree. On the other hand, I have a deep yearning for peace and harmony within me.

Mother has not been feeling well since we arrived. She stays in her room all day long. I almost wrote 'darkened room'. Isn't that funny, Gretchen? There is no darkened room in this bunker. That's impossible, as there are of course no windows. So, what I meant is a dark room, with the lights switched off. I've only been to see her once since we got here.

Later on

Gretchen, it's me again. Of course you can't hear me, but if you could you would know that I am whispering. Perhaps in order to make my whispering clear to you I should write smaller, very small. I am lying underneath two scratchy military blankets. Luckily my nightie is long enough to nearly cover my feet and I can pull the sleeves down over my hands. It also has a collar, which I have put up so that even my neck can't be touched by these awful blankets. But I digress, describe minor details – although that might perhaps be the expression of my writer's soul. Who knows? I don't want to talk to you about that now. I have to lower my voice even more and thus I will write even smaller. At the moment I am imagining you lying in a bed next to mine. No, much better: you have jumped into my bed and now we are cuddled up underneath these blankets. Whispering secrets to each other. Yes, this is what I am going to imagine. I will now switch off the torch and put my head on the pillow and imagine you are lying next to me.

Gretchen, are you sleeping? I have turned the torch back on and opened my diary again and I am continuing to write to you. My soul is heavy and you are the only one I can trust. I know you won't tell anyone else. I am scared. I can feel something terrible around us and it came with us from Schwanenwerder. I don't know how to describe it. On the one hand, I feel safe from the enemy up above. I don't really believe that the Reds will ever win. The German nation will fight to its last drop of blood. And this is certainty a nice, strong feeling. But on the other hand,

I feel something creepy behind my back, as if this place were haunted by evil ghosts who want to harm us – no, to kill us. Do you believe in ghosts, Gretchen? Do you think bad ghosts exist? Mother is in bed, weak and ill. Father attends continuous meetings. I don't think we will go on this adventure trip. I don't know why Mother said that to the little ones. Why didn't she tell them the truth? Why doesn't she tell us the truth? The truth is, we weren't safe any longer in Schwanenwerder and the only secure place for us is here, in the bunker. Why can't she explain that to the little ones? Why can't she talk to me, the eldest, about it? Sometimes I am very upset with Mother. You know that, Gretchen. And you also know that I have said mean and horrible things about Mother and Father. I wish you could speak. Does anyone else have such feelings towards their parents? Or are these feelings only inside me because I am as bad as a rotten apple? When I was still small I didn't have such feelings. Oh, it is so difficult to talk to you when you can't reply. Now I am even getting angry with you. I'd better stop writing. Good night.

IN THE BUNKER, 26 APRIL 1945

Dearest Gretchen,

Today was a wonderful day. Where shall I start? This morning, I was suddenly aware that Mother was standing at my bedside, gently waking me up. When I finally opened my eyes, all sleepy still, she announced in such a happy voice, 'My darlings, we have to prepare for a wedding!'

'Who is getting married, who is getting married?' The words spouted out of me like a water fountain.

Mother turned around to the little ones while I sat up in bed.

'It's a secret!' she said, with a lovely smile on her lips.

I knew immediately that she would tell us, that she just wanted to tease the little ones. And of course they fell for it.

'Mother, Mother, tell us, please! We won't tell anyone, honestly – Red Indian oath.'

They tried to persuade Mother in this way. She sat down next to me on the bed and asked the others to gather at our feet, to come very close.

She put her arm around me. 'Well, because you asked so nicely, I will tell you.'

She paused for a moment. Not a real pause, I could tell. When Mother feels well and doesn't suffer from these ghastly headaches, she is a wonderful actress and very funny. She raised one finger in the air.

'Listen.' Another brief pause. Then: 'The Führer will marry his Eva.'

'Oh!' Holde jumped excitedly to her feet. 'Can I be bridesmaid? Please!'

'Me too, me too!' Hedda and Heide called out together.

'We definitely need new dresses. How about pale rose with lots of lace and tulle?'

Holde was in her element. She stood up on tiptoes and performed a lovely pirouette. Mother sat next to me, smiling silently, waiting patiently until the first storm of enthusiasm had died down. But it seemed as if the three little ones had been longing for just such a game. Holde began to order Hedda and Heide around and told Helmut to get in line too. She was imagining the dresses and picturing the little flower bouquets. Mother, Hilde and I watched calmly, taking pleasure in the play of the young ones, as we three knew only too well what Mother eventually had to put into words with a heavy heart.

'The wedding will take place here in the bunker and we all have to wear what we've got.'

Holde's shoulders dropped immediately.

'Here in the bunker? But Uncle Adolf is the Führer!'

'He deserves a wonderful wedding, darling. So true. However, what do you think is more important: that our Führer celebrates a big wedding or that he is safe from the enemy?'

'But aren't we beating the enemy? Won't the war be over soon? Why can't Uncle Adolf wait?' asked Helmut.

'Miss Braun has been longing for this moment for such a long time. Now she doesn't want to postpone it any more.'

'But we still can be bridesmaids, can't we?' asked Hedda.

'I am not a bridesmaid!' Helmut said indignantly.

Oh, the little ones can be so cute. The worries they have! Mother explained that the wedding would take place the day after tomorrow. So there wouldn't be much time for preparations. Nevertheless, she would like to rehearse a canon and a choral piece. In addition Heide should recite a little poem.

'And what about me?' complained Holde, and Hedda followed like her echo: 'And me?'

'You two will get the outfits ready. We don't have much material. But do ask Miss Junge for some ribbons, which you can sew on to your skirts and blouses. And you might want to embroider the ribbons for your hair.'

'What will Miss Braun wear? A white dress with a veil?'

'No, sadly not. But still something very nice.'

'We do need to know what colour Miss Braun will wear to coordinate. A wedding has to be colour-coordinated.'

Mother moved her arm from my shoulder. I noticed that she had grown impatient with all the questions.

'Helga, please sort everything out.'

'Of course, Mother.'

'We will rehearse the songs after lunch,' Mother added, then she left the room. I knew by her slightly stooped way of walking that the headaches must have started again.

The next few hours passed in a flash. We talked to Miss Braun, who radiated happiness like the most beautiful star. We talked to Miss Junge, who was full of lovely ideas and suggestions about how to make our dresses prettier for the occasion. And in the afternoon Mother practised the songs with us.

And now I am lying here underneath the blanket writing to you. The others were so exhausted from the excitement of the day that they fell into bed over an hour ago. I only hear Hilde stirring every now and again. She sleeps in the bed above me. I must confess that it is quite strange here in the bunker. You can't really distinguish between day and night. Only the clock tells us when to sleep or when to get up. But even time doesn't really count any longer. Today, for example, Mother sent us all to bed at five. The little ones were of course dead tired and went to sleep straight away. But for me it is an unusual time to go to sleep. I am wide awake. On the other hand, this gives me the opportunity to write to you in great detail. Because there is something else I'd like to tell you. Didn't I start today's diary entry by saying what a wonderful day it had been? The news of the wedding of Uncle Adolf to Miss Braun is of course very exciting and the preparations for it are tiring and, I admit, provide a welcome change from the grey, concrete bunker days. Still, dear Gretchen, something else occurred today, something which until now only romantic novels had spoken to me about.

Love. What a huge, magnificent word – my hand shakes when I write it, my lips cannot pronounce it. I know the sort of love I have for my parents – a sublime, natural, God-given feeling, characterized by deference and gratitude. I also know the love I feel towards my siblings – a more playful feeling, like when watching cavorting little kittens. Love for the Fatherland I surely know too. Here the soul is moved more gently, as this love belongs to the heart as the hand belongs to the arm. All these loves I've just described to you, my heart knows only too well.

But every now and again I secretly dreamt of another love. A love that is written about in novels and is the subject of fairy stories. Only a few years back, when I was a silly little girl, I imagined a prince on horseback, how he would come riding towards me and lift me up onto his saddle. The fantasies of a little girl. Holde's and Hedda's heads are full of them. I, on the other hand, have started to distance myself from such girlish imaginings, especially over the last few months, since my soul and my body have started to shed their childish features. In addition, and as you may well have guessed from a hint here and there, I have toyed increasingly with the idea of entering a convent, where I can work in seclusion and submission on improving my imperfect soul and follow my desire to serve the written word. This sweet vision of my future warmed my heart. My confidence in it grew stronger with my conviction that a flawed soul such as mine couldn't expect too much from the colourful outside world. Indeed, if my expectations were too high, God could surely judge me impertinent and punish me. And now what has happened? My heart is troubled, a storm is brewing, my blood seems to be rising like the waves on the oceans, and I am unable to prevent it. My dear Gretchen, I don't know what is happening to me. My mood swings between overwhelming feelings of happiness and the darkest, deepest despair. Only yesterday, only a few hours ago, I lived a calm, contented life. Even when Mother rehearsed the songs with us, I was an innocent, perfect child. But no longer! My heart has been torn to pieces; my body is burning and no longer belongs to me. No, no, what am I saying! Dear Gretchen, don't be angry, I haven't done anything bad.

Mother had just finished rehearsing with us and left the room, when Miss Braun entered and asked me to accompany her upstairs. She told me about a temporary armistice and that we might find some flowers in the courtyard, if only dandelions and daisies, but she'd love a few fresh flowers for her wedding bouquet. I was very happy and also rather honoured that Miss Braun had chosen me to help her – of course the others wanted to come too, but Miss Braun refused their request gently but firmly, explaining that it was far too dangerous up there and they were far too little, Mother having given permission only for me. As we stepped outside our dormitory, Miss Braun indicated with a slight nod of her head a soldier who stood to one side. 'He will follow us upstairs,' she said, 'and guard us.' She slipped her arm through mine, and with jokes and smiles on our lips we climbed the stairs. Outside we were greeted by a bright blue sky. For a moment I closed my eyes, because it had been a few days since they last saw daylight. Birds were singing and only in the far distance could occasional machine-gun fire be heard. Of course the courtyard looked a mess, but I decided to ignore it, revelling in the sensation of sunshine on my face and on my skin. I started to look for little blossoms among the ruins. As I was bending down to reach the first lovely yellow dandelion, I was suddenly overcome by a sweet feeling of happiness, full of hope that the war might soon end. Faith in the eternal life of Mother Nature filled my heart. I went down on my knees in front of this lovely little flower that, although a mere weed, appeared to me to be absolutely beautiful, so beautiful that I hesitated to pick it. But then I thought about Miss Braun's shining eyes as she talked about her wedding bouquet, and thus I picked the flower. When I got up, I couldn't see Miss Braun anywhere in the courtyard, only the soldier, who stood a few metres away smoking a cigarette. I called out for her. The soldier answered instead: 'Miss Braun will be back shortly. She's just gone to fetch a sun hat.' I thanked him hastily without looking at him. The soldier and I were left alone in the courtyard. For a brief moment I felt uncomfortable. But then I reasoned with myself: it was broad daylight, Miss Braun would be back shortly. As I bent down towards another flower, I heard the soldier's voice once again. 'May I have a conversation with you?' he asked. I stood up immediately. The soldier had moved closer but still kept an appropriate distance. I realized that he was probably only two or three years older than me. A shy smile played on his lips. Of course I could have denied him a conversation. Should I have done so? Oh, if only I were truly pure and virtuous, as I've always pretended to you I am, I would not have talked to him. And here I am trying to find reasons why I allowed him to talk to me. Was it because of the blue sky, the sun, the flowers – the happiness I felt up there in the fresh air, having escaped, if only for a moment, from those hulking grey walls? I said yes. And he told me he knew me from Schwanenwerder – in the last few months, he had been on guard duty outside our house for a couple of weeks. Often at night-time. He had seen light shining from my window. Did I like to read and write? he asked me. I nodded bashfully. He then told me that he too likes to write and if I wanted to hear the stories he had written he could read them to me some day. Oh, Gretchen, it was like a dream as we strolled across the yard. Part of me expected to wake up at any moment, and the longer we talked the less I wanted to wake up. And though at the outset I had hoped for the quick return of Miss Braun, thoughts of my dear friend, without whom I wouldn't have had this lovely outing, faded with every step. I glanced at my companion. Thick blond hair swept across a high forehead. A strong nose accentuating a regular face and a beautifully curved mouth smiling down on me. But the most agreeable feature is his bright blue eyes – each time I looked up they seemed to rest on me as if I were the most wonderful creature they had ever seen. His gaze gave me courage and I opened my heart to him and told him about my poetic soul. I don't know how long we strolled up and down the courtyard. Sometimes we stopped, he would look at me, I would glance shyly up to him. Eventually we heard Miss Braun's adorable laugh as she came up the stairs. 'My name is Knut,' he said quickly. And I gave him my name, which he repeated gently. 'Helga. May I hope for a continuation of our conversation?' he asked. I nodded, turned around and ran towards Miss Braun, whose pretty head was now adorned by a sun hat. I slipped my arm under hers and told her about the lovely flowers I was holding in my hand. I am sure that I spoke with far too much enthusiasm and she may even have started to wonder what had happened to the former Helga, whose dark sad soul had suddenly taken flight like a butterfly. Yes, that is how my soul now appears to me, like a butterfly that hovers above a beautiful spring meadow, performing a sacred sun dance. There is no more war, no more destruction and devastation, no more fear of drunken soldiers, fear for my life. No more hulking grey walls, no more living underground with no windows to let the sun and moon shine in. All of this is no more, has vanished into thin air. And all because Knut plucked up the courage to address me and I forgot for a few minutes my maidenly reserve. Is this the love that books and poems talk about? If it is, then it is a thousand times more beautiful in real life than on paper.

Dear Gretchen, please don't be sad, but I now must quickly go to bed. I have written so much that my hand is hurting and tomorrow will be quite a tiring day because of all the wedding preparations. Good night.

IN THE BUNKER, 27 APRIL 1945

Dearest Gretchen,

Is love physical? Does true romantic love, as the poets describe it, reside within the body? Oh, if only you could answer me. Something quite strange is happening to me, has taken control of me. Yes, my entire being is possessed by it – my soul, my feelings, my mind, my head – my body is trembling and shaking, as if inside I've developed wings, am stretching them. I try to keep my hand steady while I write to you, forcing myself to concentrate on the actual words flowing out of my pen and onto the paper. Please, dear Gretchen, forgive me, but I find it incredibly hard to write to you, to talk to you, to reveal my heart to you. What is happening with me? Why am I not overcome by calm romantic feelings instead of this tremor that runs through my body? Has it something to do with my imperfection? Am I like an animal that merely reacts with its body? I now live only for the moments when I can see him – Knut. We were in the courtyard again today. Once again, Miss Braun had asked me to accompany her upstairs. Again Knut followed us, and as soon as we reached the outside, Miss Braun sent the three other soldiers, who were standing around, downstairs and then, putting her hand to her forehead, as if she'd forgotten something, she walked off too, merely saying over her shoulder that she'd be back in a moment or two. Knut sidled next to me and his hand touched mine fleetingly, as if by accident. I thought my body was going to splinter into a thousand pieces. We walked slowly side by side, talking about Goethe and Novalis, and he told me about a woman writer called Günderrode. She was a famous poetess, he told me, but had died young. I tried to listen to what he said, wanted to reply in an intelligent manner, but my mind, my entire head, was enveloped in a thick fog and I could only feel and think about my body. My body is now guiding me – oh, dear Gretchen, am I a bad person? It's my body that wants to be with Knut; it's my body that doesn't want to live without him any more. Knut suddenly took my hand and pulled me into the shadow of a doorway. 'Helga, may I kiss you?' he asked. I nodded, of course I nodded: my body nodded, my soul nodded, my heart nodded. And he placed his lips on mine and for a while we remained like this. And I felt my lips tremble. And then my body pushed against his and my lips opened. No, no, no, I don't want to continue. I am such a sinful person. You will get the wrong impression. I long to tell you how shy and sweet and innocent I am. Oh, if only I could! Suddenly we heard Miss Braun calling for me. We jumped apart and when I reached her she immediately started telling me how she'd spent the whole night writing invitations for her wedding tomorrow. Even though she knows that no one will be able to come, she desires to share her joy with all her friends. But when the Führer realized what she was doing, he became very angry. He prefers the idea of a small wedding. That's how he always imagined it. So she took the invitations and simply burned them. Because what counts is not the size of the wedding, but that she will now be joined with the Führer for ever. Afterwards we continued our stroll in silence. Once again she had put her arm in mine. Like two best friends. I was a bit worried that Mother could see us, because I know that she isn't always very fond of Miss Braun. Fickle and vulgar, says Mother. When we stopped for a moment, Miss Braun let go of my arm and pulled out her packet of cigarettes, offering me one. I shook my head. 'You are right,' Miss Braun said, after she lit one for herself. 'You are such a sensible girl – no, a sensible young lady, that's what you are now. My goodness, I still remember you as a little girl with two pigtails.' We were standing face to face. If it hadn't been for the smoke, I could have sworn that she had tears in her eyes. Suddenly she took my chin in the palm of her free hand. 'Do you love Knut?' she asked. Her question startled me; I didn't know how to answer. How did she know his first name? Suddenly I was frightened – I didn't want to get him into trouble. She must have sensed how scared I was. She let go of my chin. 'Knut is the son of an acquaintance of my sister,' she said. 'That's why he is here and not at the front. Here he is safe. He is a good boy.' We started walking again. I looked around me surreptitiously, but couldn't see Knut anywhere. 'He loves you,' Miss Braun continued. 'You can trust him, Helga.' I began to feel hot, so hot that my head felt like a burning oven that might explode at any moment. I nodded, not feeling at all well. Then suddenly her mood changed. She tossed away her cigarette, grasped both of my hands and started to dance around me, twirling me about in a circle. 'Children, children, how amazing life is,' she called out, full of joy. 'And as long as you are young, ah, how wonderful!' While still twirling, she threw her head back. 'Helga, enjoy life. There is nothing better than life.' And she put her arm around me and for a short while we danced in a tight embrace.

I like Miss Braun. Yes, I like her. And I don't care what Mother says. Mother isn't always right. No, she definitely isn't.

IN THE BUNKER, 28 APRIL 1945

Dearest Gretchen,

I've become so fickle, so incredibly fickle. In the past I was deeply rooted. My belief in my vocation, to live my life quietly in a convent, grateful that I – such an imperfect creature – was allowed to be part of this life at all. A passion for poetic expression used to live in the depths of my soul, but whenever that passion was on the brink of surfacing, fear and guilt reminded me of the dangers of empty dreams. Of course I understood that my poetic aspirations were nothing more than dreams. But now there is a burning sensation in my breast, in my belly, spreading through my entire body. I no longer see myself through my own eyes but through Knut's. And Knut regards me as a poet and as the fairest and sweetest creature he's ever laid eyes on. And yet, even as I write these words down for you – you, my most loyal friend – I know that they are not true. I am not the one Knut sees. But oh, Gretchen, as soon as I put the pen down and turn away from these sheets of paper, as soon as I can hope to meet Knut, perhaps even in the corridor outside the door, I am again, in my own mind, the way he sees me. I want to stay very close to him so that the truth about my imperfection will never come between us.

My days now consist only of the moments when I can see Knut. Miss Braun – I am now allowed to call her Eva – is so sweet. Earlier on she permitted us to be alone in her room for a short while. I didn't want to talk; I only wanted to place my lips on his. But he took my hands and held them in his and said, 'We need to get away. It is too dangerous here.' I tried to calm him. No, he shouldn't worry, Father wouldn't punish him, and Miss Braun would surely not tell on us. His reply was very strange indeed. No, it wasn't he who was in danger, but I. Of course I laughed and told him, 'I feel totally safe here. Father, the Führer, all the most important men of the country are gathered here and the war is nearly won.' He just looked at me for a very long time and inside me I had the feeling I was falling into a big black hole. 'Helga, the war is lost,' he said then. 'We have surrendered and . . .' He was about to continue. I looked at him, I saw his lips moving and I leant forward and kissed him. I just wanted to kiss him; I didn't want to talk. At first Knut responded to my kiss. But then he backed off. 'We have to get out of here, Helga. Come with me!'

Gretchen, dear Gretchen, what shall I do? I can't run away. How could I leave Mother and Father and the dear little ones? I am sure we all are very safe here. I don't know if we have won or lost the war. But Uncle Adolf and Eva have married today. Mother put on her best dress. Such excitement! The wedding was eventually celebrated with just a few guests. Mother and Father were there – we, however, weren't allowed to attend after all. The Führer didn't even want to listen to our little choir. Of course Mother was sad about it. Only Eva was happy and laughed and told us not to worry. 'You know what the Führer is like,' she said. 'What he decides, he does. And he decided a long time ago to celebrate his wedding with a very small circle of friends. And that's what he will do.' And then Miss Braun, I mean Eva, asked Mother if we couldn't sing just for her. I could tell from Mother's pursed lips that she thought this idea was ridiculous. But the little ones were already clinging to Mother's skirt, begging her. So we sang. The little ones have now finally gone to sleep. I can hear only Helmut beneath his blankets, secretly shooting cowboys. One of the soldiers carved a few figurines for him. That's how kind they all are to us.

IN THE BUNKER, 29 APRIL 1945

Dearest Gretchen,

I just don't know what to do. A deep abyss has opened up inside me, has divided my whole being in two. You are the only one I can tell: I love Knut so deeply and intensely that I can hardly bear to be apart from him. I know I want to stay with him for ever. I can't live without him any more. With him I will go through life, endure life – only in his arms will I be happy. What was my life like before, without him? I cannot remember. Knut is now my life. My heart tells me that, my heart needs him, otherwise it would fall to pieces. Only in his presence am I calm. Only in his presence am I safe. That is one side of the abyss. When I stand on the other side, where my dear parents and my darling brother and sweet sisters are, I am overcome by feelings of guilt that paralyse me and would have me believe that peace can only be found on their side. I am jumping from one side to the other across a deep, yawning crevasse. I still have the power. But for how long? Gretchen! For how much longer? And what will happen then? Will I fall into the crevasse, be swallowed up by nothingness? Knut keeps insisting that I come with him. We spend more and more time with each other. We are always bumping into each other in the long corridors, finding a niche, a dark corner. No one really cares any more. No one even notices. Mother's headaches worsened again, unbearable pain keeps her in bed. Father spends all his time with Uncle Adolf. The little ones are in the kitchen with Miss Junge. They like it there. I think it reminds them of Schwanenwerder and the lovely Bertha, whom they all miss so badly. Her calm nature, her warm soft hugs. Here in the bunker a continuous coming and going prevails; they even bring the injured down here now. But for me, dear Gretchen, these wounded people, this chaos, this noise, all mean bliss. Because of them Knut and I are left alone. Just imagine if we were still in Schwanenwerder! I would be sitting on the swings like a little girl longing for a prince to come. Knut would never have dared talk to me; he would have been too frightened of provoking Father's anger. Just imagine – Knut would have never talked to me! We would never have found each other! But we had to find each other. It was our destiny. That's why we are all here in the bunker. And my heart rejoices. Yes, dear Gretchen, my heart rejoices. I would love to spend all my time in his arms. We can talk about future plans tomorrow. But Knut keeps on talking: 'We have to leave,' he says. Because of me, he says, we have to leave. I, Helga, will no longer be safe here. 'And up there it is safer?' I ask him, laughing. Yes, I laugh, because all I feel is happiness and endless love when I am with him. 'Yes,' he replies, 'for you it would be safer up there.' His friends are able to help us. He knows how we can get out of Berlin. He is very serious and indeed reminds me of my brother, who is also very serious when he fights against bad cowboys. Sometimes I watch Helmut sneaking on tiptoe through the corridors with his tomahawk in one hand and his big colourful headdress. The soldiers laugh about him, they make jokes behind his back, these drunken men, but Helmut doesn't notice, that's how engrossed he is in his game. Dear Gretchen, I wish Knut would stop talking. Everything would be easier then. Because I wish for nothing more than to unite my two worlds. I don't want to hurt anyone, neither Father nor Mother, and also not my dear brother and sisters. But definitely not Knut. I would never hurt him. I love him. I would give my life for him. My life!

Later on

Oh, Gretchen! What is happening with me? I am sitting

here crying my eyes out. I've run away from Knut; he tried to hold me back and grabbed my wrist, but I managed to escape. He is standing outside the door, begging me to open it. He said something truly horrible. Father and Mother want to kill themselves and us, the little ones and me. How can he say something like this? He wants to force me to come with him. But now I really can't go with him, if he hates my family so much!

IN THE BUNKER, 30 APRIL 1945

Dearest Gretchen,

I have never wished more fervently to be older than I do now. Of course I cannot marry Knut yet, we will have to wait at least two more years. We have promised each other that we will get engaged in two years. The war will soon be over – and Gretchen, I have to be quite honest with you, I don't really mind if we win or lose. Father of course must never hear me say that, because he wanted so badly to see the German nation – his nation – win, and of course I am frightened of the Bolsheviks and the Communists. But, I wonder more and more, aren't they humans too? Are they really that awful? Oh, Gretchen, my heart is so small, because it has room for nothing but my own personal happiness. And this happiness comprises my family and Knut. And I want nothing else except to live in peace and happiness with him. I am already imagining our little home, just a tiny house and a garden with gnarled old apple trees. I see the apple trees in full blossom and myself in front of the house holding our first child in my arms. I am standing there and with my free arm I am waving to Knut. For this dream of a loving home with Knut, I am willing to sacrifice my dream of becoming a poet. Knut, however, would like me to study. His idea is that we will study together. Today we didn't talk about running away but imagined instead how it will be when we are living together. And we stopped talking and held each other silently. And then he told me that whatever happens he will not leave me. Yesterday he pushed a note under the door. He was sorry, he wrote, that he had been angry with my parents. It wasn't true what he had said. He would never try to force me to go with him again. Afterwards we hid in the larder and sat there almost the entire night; we just sat there very close together.

Later on

Gretchen? Are you sleeping? I can't sleep and I almost can't write. I am crying so much, I can't keep still. I wanted to leave the room, but the door is locked. Two hours ago when I sneaked in it was still open. Hilde, Helmut and the little ones were already sleeping soundly. I didn't want to leave Knut, but he thought I'd better sleep a little. He said we shouldn't sit all night in the cold larder. What if we fell asleep and someone found us the next morning? We'd get into real trouble. In my room I sat down to write to you. Suddenly a heaviness descended upon my heart. A terrible fear came over me while completing the last sentences. I lay down in bed and just wanted to close my eyes and fall asleep, but I felt as if I were the only person on earth and terror grabbed hold of me. What if Knut had died? And so I had only one thought – I had to find him. But oh dear, oh dear . . . the door . . . it is locked. Why? Who locked it? I didn't hear anything. When will it be opened again? I am so terribly frightened. I lie underneath the blankets, my torch is flickering; soon it will stop working and I won't be able to continue to write. Gretchen, what am I going to do? Where is Knut? Does he know we are locked in our room?

Gretchen? I've tried to sleep again, but I can't. I just have to cry, I am so lost, I am so full of despair. What if everybody out there is dead and we are the only survivors? I listened at the door – no sound, no movement from outside. Total silence. Not even some distant shouting from a drunken soldier. We don't have any food in here and I am sure the air conditioning will stop at some point. What then? How can I save the little ones? I can't save them. We will all suffocate. No, no, I shouldn't think like that, absolutely not. It is for our own sakes that we are locked in here. Surely Father or Mother . . . yes, Father locked us in here, to protect us from all the bad people outside. Father and Mother want to protect us; they don't want to harm us. We are their children. You are the most precious things I have, Mother said. Mother has a heart of gold. How proudly she used to show us off. Mother of the Nation, Mother of the German Nation! So proud she used to be, still is. No one would ever be allowed to harm us; she wouldn't let that happen. She's always been very protective of us. I would have loved to continue going to school, but she thought it better to have teachers come to Schwanenwerder. She said that was safer.

Oh, Gretchen, I can't go to sleep. I just can't. All my powers of expression are gone. All my pious feelings have gone. Only terrible fear is left, keeping me awake.

Dear Knut, these words are for you. Are you still alive? Where are you? Please come and save me. Please.

I am so silly – so truly silly and also so terribly happy. I write in haste. We are alive! Father has just unlocked the door! He had locked it secretly last night. I flew into his arms. I love him. I have to eat breakfast and then I will look for Knut. Father said it won't take long now and everything will be over, we shouldn't worry at all.

IN THE BUNKER, 1 MAY 1945

Dearest Gretchen,

I just started a letter to you and then tore it up again, although I once promised you I would never tear any pages out of my diary, but would cherish every single word I ever addressed to you. Now I have broken that promise. Because what I alluded to was simply too ghastly and horrible to leave on the page. I prefer to talk about the pleasant side of our lives down here in the bunker and will now describe to you the charming scene which is presenting itself to me right this very moment. I wish I could paint – I would sketch you a lovely picture. We are in the kitchen. At one end of the table the three little ones are sitting with Miss Junge, playing *Mensch ärgere Dich nicht*. Heide has just burst into tears because Holde kicked her figurine out of the game. She is now sitting on Miss Junge's lap, sobbing. Helmut and a soldier are sitting at the other end of the table, carving little horses out of wood. Helmut's intense concentration shows: he is bent deep over his work, tongue between his teeth. Hilde is sitting at the little sewing table, under a low-hanging light bulb. She is reading. Since we arrived in the bunker, she seems to be reading non-stop. I really don't know where she is getting all the books from. I am sitting next to the oven. The stovepipe is burning hot and providing warmth. I am balancing my notebook on my knees. Therefore please forgive me if my handwriting is a bit shaky today. I haven't seen Father since this morning and Mother appears to be feeling better. Earlier on she visited us briefly. She looked very nice in her blue dress. Her cheeks were coloured and her eyes bright. She proudly showed us a decoration that the Führer had awarded her. She hugged each one of us and kissed us and said that without us she would never have attained such honour in the eyes of the Führer.

Of course, dear Gretchen, I know full well whose name I haven't mentioned and whose description you are waiting for. Because I have mentioned all of my loved ones except one. I haven't seen him. After breakfast I searched for him everywhere. Finally I was so desperate that I dared to ask two of his colleagues. Sergeant Knut? Did I know his surname? They had never heard of a Knut. Oh, Gretchen, you cannot imagine how I felt. As if the earth had swallowed him. Suddenly I wondered if I might have just dreamt it all. I ran back into our room and searched for my notebook underneath the mattress and found everything I had written to you about Knut. So I was reassured – I hadn't dreamt it. I beg you not to think of me as losing my mind, though sometimes it is very difficult to keep day and night, dream and reality, apart down here. For days I haven't slept properly and last night not at all. The air is becoming worse too. Our fight for survival demands huge sacrifices. After I had reassured myself that Knut had not been just a dream, I plucked up all my courage and knocked on Miss Braun's – no, Eva Hitler's – door. No answer. Instead Miss Junge came running towards me. Frau Hitler wasn't feeling well, she told me. She took me by the hand and pulled me away. Suddenly I could no longer hold back my tears. The kind Miss Junge led me into her room and sat me down on her bed as if I were a little child. She pulled a chair close and took my hands between hers. I poured my heart out to her. Miss Junge listened, stroking my hair every now and then. After I had finished she looked at me compassionately. Then she said, 'You are experiencing your first heartache, Helga, my lovely.' 'It is unbearably painful,' I cried out. She took me in her arms and rocked me gently back and forth like a little child and for a moment my tormented soul was given some respite. But eventually I freed myself from her. I had to face reality – that, at least, I owed myself. 'Do you know where Knut could be?' She wanted to pull me back into her arms, but this time I resisted. I didn't look at her – my sight was blurred by too many tears – I kept my eyes fixed on my lap, where I saw as if through a veil my hands clasped in desperation. I think I heard her take a deep breath before she put the knife into my chest as I had asked her to.

'I heard that Private Schneider, Knut Schneider, has deserted.'

My head sank down into my hands. I would have loved to die then.

My dear Gretchen, I feel quite strange. My soul finds it hard to follow what has happened to me. Can I have misjudged another human being in such a way? Only yesterday we made plans for a future together. And now he is gone, as if he had never existed. Everything inside me is flat. No wind ripples the water. The crevasse has gone too. No peaks and depths exist inside me. What is the meaning of all this, Gretchen? Does it mean I am not capable of romantic feelings, that I have no capacity for the all-consuming pains of love? An artist, a poet needs to experience lows and highs in order to describe them. Father knows how to experience lows and highs, he is a true poet, and when he was younger he used to write novels. I am only his daughter; my vocation is a far lesser one. Dear Gretchen, I am sitting here close to the warm stove and around me are gathered my loved ones. The little ones need me. Mother is ill and too weak to spend much time with them, to care for them much. My place is here; this is where my duty lies. And when the little ones have grown up into decent, honest people, I shall then enter the convent. A flawed soul like mine cannot, should not, expect much from life. I am very pleased, dear Gretchen, that I've got you, that you are mine whatever happens. I can tell you everything. I know you forgive me and that you condone my childish, naïve feelings for that youth. Does every woman have to wade through such floods of emotion while growing up?

Knut exploited my weaknesses, my romantic longings, and separated me from my family. He, who no longer has a family of his own, couldn't bear the sight of happy, blessed intimacy. How blemished I am, even to have ever contemplated leaving my family and to have ever doubted Mother and Father's innocence. How awful of me! I will make up for it and reassure them for the rest of my life of my eternal love for them.

THE PILLBOX

Miss Junge has called them into the kitchen, but leaves as soon as they arrive. 'Children, I just have to finish typing something for your father.' Their mother stands in front of the cooker, where a big pan of milk is heating. Once more she looks pale and ill. Helga notices immediately that she is suffering from her headaches again.

'Mother, please go to bed. I can give the little ones their milk.'

'No!' Magda almost shouts, turning round abruptly to face her eldest daughter, hiding the cooker behind her back as if she wants to prevent Helga from coming closer. Then she continues in a calmer voice: 'Today I will heat the milk for you.'

The children sit down quietly around the table. They are exhausted. The bad air in the bunker is taking its toll. Magda removes the boiling milk from the cooker, pours it into the six cups standing next to the sink. She puts a full cup in front of each child.

'I don't drink milk any more,' says Helga. 'You know that.' And she pushes the cup away.

'It is important to drink milk, especially at your age.' Magda is irritated.

The other children have already lowered their noses towards the milk. They blow on it and start to drink.

'What delicious milk you made us today,' Heide shouts out enthusiastically. 'So sweet.'

Magda smiles, leans across the table and gently strokes the pale cheek of her youngest.

'I put twice as much honey in it today.'

Helga's stomach convulses. The smell of the sweet milk invades her nostrils. She suppresses an urge to retch. She never used to like milk much but in the last few months she has started to be repulsed by it. The mere thought of the skin forming on top and the possibility of feeling the loose, slimy thing on her lips makes her shiver with disgust.

'Helga, drink your milk,' her mother commands again.

Helga's eyes fill with tears. She sits in front of the milk with her head lowered and her hands folded in her lap. She tries not to breathe through her nose, shuffling towards the edge of the kitchen bench, hoping that her mother hasn't noticed.

'My God, stop making such a fuss!' Magda is losing her patience – Helga can tell because of the shrill voice. She doesn't want to upset her mother. She knows her mother is suffering from headaches. She really wants to help her. To be a good daughter. Especially now, since Knut has gone, she wants to make up.

'I haven't drunk milk for a long time,' she pleads.

Hilde helps her out.

'That's true. She drinks peppermint tea now.'

'We don't have peppermint tea here,' Magda replies

sharply. 'I have managed to get you this milk today. Father's soldiers – young men – have risked their lives for it, because I wanted to be nice to you.'

Magda walks around the table, takes Helga's cup and holds it to her mouth.

'Drink!'

Tears are now streaming down the girl's cheeks. But she keeps her lips tightly closed, so as not to let in the liquid and prevent herself from retching. Silently, she burps and tastes bile. She feels her mother's hand grabbing her neck, bending her head backwards. Once again the cup is forced to her closed mouth.

'Drink! It's good for you.'

For a short moment Helga looks into her mother's face – it seems to her as pale as a ghost. She hears one of the little ones – Heide? – crying. And she hears either Holde or Hedda begging their mother, 'Please let her be. She doesn't drink milk.' Helga closes her eyes, the cup hits hard against her teeth, she opens her mouth, tastes the salt of her tears, then the thick white liquid. She begins to cough, she burps, undigested food rising in her throat while the milk makes its way down. The grip loosens from her neck. Helga leans forward and throws up milk and food remains in one single torrent.

When Helga suddenly lurched forward, the cup fell out of Magda's hand. Magda stares at the thick puddle on the table. The sound of crying children reaches her from far away. A desperate voice pleads, 'Mother, please!' There is a wild drumming in Magda's head. The headache has now settled right in the middle of her skull. Normally it lives above the right eye, where it hammers so hard against her cranium that the vibration from the pain spreads through her entire head and body, right down to the stomach. But now someone has set off artillery – in the very centre of her brain. She has to pull herself together. She has frightened the children. That shouldn't be. She only wanted to be nice to them. But she didn't reckon with Helga's stubbornness.

'Mother!' Heide is suddenly standing next to her, throwing her little arms around her thighs, pressing her tiny face against Magda's hips. 'Mother, Helga is not feeling well,' sobs her youngest. 'Let her be. She doesn't feel well at all.'

Magda's body straightens. She strokes Heide's hair and decides to ignore the pain in her head. 'Don't worry, my darling.' She frees herself from Heide's embrace, leaning down to Helga, who is still sitting at the table, crying. She pulls up her eldest and leads her to the sink. She turns on the water and washes her daughter's face. Helga doesn't resist.

'Tomorrow I'll get you peppermint tea.'

She straightens the cardigan on the girl's shoulders and places a tender kiss on her daughter's forehead. Helga must have grown one or two centimetres in the last week. They are now the same height.

'Hilde, take your sister and the little ones and get ready for bed. I will quickly clean up here and then come and read you a bedtime story.'

Hilde touches Helga's arm and leads her towards the door. A sour taste lingers in Helga's mouth. The children scurry through the corridor. Everything appears strangely calm and quiet, despite a lot of panic throughout the day and more coming and going than usual. Miss Junge had even forgotten to prepare their lunch until Helmut found her and asked for a few sandwiches. Continuous reverberations from above had numbed the senses when suddenly an ear-splitting sound tore apart the stuffy, stagnant air in the bunker, just as they sat down in Miss Junge's room to eat.

'That must have been a bullseye,' Helmut shouted. Helga was amazed by her brother's continued enthusiasm for the war. To her mind it wasn't at all clear for whom this could have been a successful hit – for them or for the enemy. Miss Junge jumped to her feet, opened the door slightly and immediately shut it again.

'Everything's fine.' She sat down and bit into her bread. Then she opened the jar with the cherries that stood on the table. They talked about the summer and how many cherry earrings one could actually hang on one ear.

Now everything is quiet. Two soldiers are sleeping in a corner – they smell of schnapps – otherwise, no living soul makes an appearance. In their room the little ones undress without fuss, get into their nightclothes and are already in their beds. Helga can still feel Mother's grip on her neck and the cup pressing against her teeth. Her jaw hurts. A quick thought about her diary. She wanted to write. She too takes off her clothes, puts on her nightdress and gets into bed. No one brushed their teeth. Helga is too tired to dwell on it further, let alone do anything about it. She turns onto her side, facing the wall.

Hilde says, 'Good night, Helga, sleep well. I am sure you will feel better tomorrow.'

'Night-night, Hilde.'

Magda stands at the kitchen table, staring at her daughter's vomit. Helmut was the last one to leave the kitchen. He had already shut the door behind him, but then he pushed it open once more and put his head around the corner.

'Mother, can I help you?'

Magda shook her head, smiling. What a lovely boy!

'No, my Indian chief.'

'You will come to our room afterwards, won't you?' Helmut asked in a worried voice. 'I mean, before you go back to your room. Won't you?'

'Of course I will come. I've promised.'

'Good,' he said, reassured. 'I will wait for you, because I want to tell you something.'

'Don't you want to tell me now?'

'No,' came his firm reply. 'It is a secret and I can only whisper it to you in bed. Miss Junge said so. I'll see you in a while, then.' And his head disappeared. The door swung shut.

Magda stirs herself, goes to the sink, takes a cloth, goes back to the table, stands still for a moment, indecisive, shakes her head, surprised at herself, returns to the sink, takes the bucket from underneath the sink, fills it with a little water, just enough to cover the bottom, heads to the table and, with a sweeping motion, wipes the mess into the bucket. She bends down and cleans the worst off the floor too. Then she pours the thick liquid into the sink, again lets the water run into the bucket, this time mixed with soap. She scrubs the table and floor vigorously. The strong reek begins to dissipate. She has used the same cloth for the table and the floor, the washing-up cloth with which she will now clean the cups since there is no scrubbing brush. A lame excuse! This is disgusting and unhygienic. Times have changed. It used to be merely simple, plain dirt that entered the house on the soles of the feet. But nowadays! The enemy stands at the threshold, germs and bacteria are spreading. None of her children has the most robust health. They are often deathly pale with deep shadows under their eyes, even though she is trying her best, considering the circumstances, always paying particular attention to their eating. No. Even if her children never enter this kitchen again, she has no right to let herself go. She tears open the kitchen cupboards one after the other. She finds unused cleaning cloths and three enamel basins. She has to go to the children tonight, but the cleaning won't take long and the activity will give her the inner peace which she so desperately needs. She closes the cupboard doors. She will only wipe the surfaces. Whoever enters the kitchen after her will find a clean, well-organized room. They didn't flee in a hurry, didn't abandon everything in disarray out of fear of the enemy. There is no way that she will leave such an impression. She wipes the table once more. She gives it another good scrub, with lots of water and soap suds. She is happy to be able to take her children with her. She stops, sits down on a chair, pushing a strand of hair out of her face. She places the wet cloth on the table and pulls the pillbox out of her skirt pocket. The lid springs open. There they lie, seven capsules next to each other, seven little saviours. She closes the lid again, puts the box back into her pocket. She continues with the task she has set herself. The cooker is the next item on her mental list. Thank God it is quite clean, needs only a wipe down. She inspects the kitchen with satisfaction. She takes the little vase with the two daffodils from the sideboard and places it in the middle of the table. Beautiful. She has left the floor till last. She starts with the corner next to the sink, because it is the farthest away from the door. Underneath the cooker, beneath the table, only she doesn't put up the chairs, as she wants to avoid having to walk across the wet floor in order to put them down again after finishing with the mopping. The floor has to be clean and smooth, without any marks. She pushes the bench and chairs under the table. Decent people sat here, not barbarians. At the door, she turns around one last time. The floor is wet and shiny. A fresh smell of soap lingers in the air. She turns the light off, takes the bucket and mop and closes the door behind her. In the bathroom she pours the dirty water into the toilet, placing the bucket and mop in the corner. She glances quickly at herself in the mirror, out of habit. She rolls down the sleeves of her blouse and straightens her skirt.

The children's room is quiet. As she had hoped, they left the dim emergency light burning, expecting their mother to follow and read them a story. Magda closes the door behind her, her eyes adjusting to the poor light. Will one of the children move, open their eyes, ask for her? But the room remains silent. No one stirs. The sleeping mixture that Magda had put into their milk has done its job. The children have fallen quickly into a deep sleep. Even Helga. Magda breathes a sigh of relief.

Helga hears a rustling. She lies in her bed facing the wall, covered with two scratchy blankets up to her nose. Legs bent, pulled tight to her chest. Someone has entered the room, but she keeps her eyes closed, breathing slowly, and hopes that it sounds as if she is asleep. Her first thought was her mother. The way the door handle was pushed down, with quiet determination. Helga had wanted to turn around, had wanted to call out, 'Mother?', but a sudden, vague feeling had held her back. For a moment she couldn't even say with certainty that someone had entered the room. The door had been opened and closed again. Had Mother looked in only for a moment? If it had really been her mother who entered the room, she would by now have moved. Helga hears the humming of the generator. It is pitch black behind her closed eyelids. The blanket gives her a sense of security. She holds it tightly from the inside, with both hands, folded as if in prayer, pushing it gently against her upper lip so that she is able to open her mouth beneath the blanket, slowly breathing in and out.

Knut. He might have come back, drunk, desperately longing for her. He had a drink to pluck up courage. But he didn't really want to face her in a drunken state; he wanted to sleep first and by accident got the wrong door, the door he had stood in front of only two days ago. Now he is in the room. And slowly he understands. He has entered the room of his sweetheart. He feels sweaty and wishes he were sober. He feels dizzy and has to hold on to the door frame.

He is approaching her bed, yes, Helga can hear it. There is no doubt: someone is in the room and it might be Knut. Someone is now standing right next to her bed and it might be Knut. He is looking at her. His beloved. In her sleep she resembles an angel. If only she'd turn around, open her eyes. Helga has seen it in movies, like Zarah Leander, in her lace nightdress, sleepy, her hair spread out on a white pillow. Soon any moment now, Knut, delighted, in love, will bend down and kiss her. And she won't resist, she won't be embarrassed, she will respond to his kiss. If only she'd turn around. Then it will all become reality.

But Helga doesn't turn around. Someone is standing next to her bed, staring down at her. Now a chair is being moved, carefully, quietly, not as if knocked about in a drunken state. And suddenly Helga is sure that her mother has entered the room. After all, Mother wanted to come and say good night. It's not Knut. A sharp disappointment cuts into Helga's heart. She opens her eyes slowly, her eyelids heavy. Then. The rustling of paper, as if someone is leafing through a book. She immediately shuts her eyes again.

For a moment Helga hears nothing but the pounding of her heart.

Her diary! Earlier she had taken it from under her mattress; she had wanted to write, but they were called into the kitchen and she had had to hide the book quickly under the blanket. And, when she got into bed, she had put it on the table. She should have put it back under the mattress, but she was too exhausted from vomiting to feel up to lifting the heavy mattress and putting the diary back there.

'You are not allowed to look at it,' she had told Hilde.

'I don't need your diary. I've got far better books,' Hilde had replied, quick-witted as ever.

Helga had left the diary on the table. Never before had she been so careless with it. Never. And Mother is surely leafing through it now. And she will know everything. Everything! Especially about Knut. What will she think about her daughter? And Miss Braun! Mother will have an even lower opinion of Miss Braun. Mother will surely tell Father. The disappointment on his face! But Helga hasn't committed any crime. They will think she is far too young! Oh, she knows her body is sinful. But she hasn't done anything. Now she definitely can't just open her eyes, absolutely not. By doing so she would reveal herself, reveal how fake she was, how she'd betrayed her mother by pretending to sleep. A trickster. A liar. Mother wouldn't understand. Helga's eyes are beginning to fill with tears. She can't let it happen! What if she then starts to tremble? How long will Mother stay? Mother is getting up. She didn't read the diary for long. Perhaps she didn't read the diary at all? Oh, Helga is so confused. She suddenly feels the concrete walls, the metre-thick ceiling, the earth – all pushing down on her. She needs fresh air, she wants to sit again on the swings in the garden of Schwanenwerder, she wants to run across a huge green meadow under an infinite blue sky. This bunker is suffocating her. She hasn't seen the sky for three days now, hasn't smelt the fresh air, hasn't breathed it in. No, whatever it is that lay on the table, it wasn't her diary. That is here with her in her bed. She pushed it under the blanket. It lies at her feet. If she were to stretch her legs she could feel it. She could move a bit. Even sleeping people move. That is quite normal.

If only Mother would leave now. But she doesn't leave. She is moving about behind Helga's back. What is she doing? A short, sharp metallic sound. Helga's right eye twitches. It is difficult to keep your eyes shut without screwing them up. Mother is moving near the beds of the small ones, behind Helga's back. There, the clicking sound again, followed by Mother's deep breathing. Helga knows that clicking sound. She knows it as well as the smell of her mother. The sound of Mother's little pillbox opening. Mother holds it in her right hand, her thumb pushes down the tiny lever and the lid jumps open. With the left hand she takes out a pill, or sometimes a capsule, and pushes the lid closed again with the thumb – click, there it is, a quick click – and in one flowing movement she puts the little box back into her jacket pocket or her handbag, having placed the pill in her mouth, and reaches with her empty right hand for the water glass. A series of actions which is as much part of her mother as the headaches. But never before has she opened the box repeatedly and at such short intervals. Bedsprings squeak. It's Heide's or Hedda's bed. Mother must have sat down. Click. This time, however, it sounded more like two stones striking each other. Or teeth snapping shut.

Mother also owns two round porcelain pillboxes; embroidered cloth covers their lids. But she prefers to use the metal one, which is slightly bigger and oval in shape. In Schwanenwerder it lived on Mother's bedside table. Before her closed eyes, Helga now sees herself pushing open the door to her mother's bedroom. But Mother isn't lying in her bed. Helga stands in the doorway, forgetting to breathe, petrified. She was always worried about her mother, frightened that she wouldn't be there one day. Then the girl's eyes fall on the bedside table. The pillbox. Helga is able to breathe again and now she hears water running in the bathroom. Mother is feeling better. Helga shuts the door quietly.

'Your mother is different from other mothers,' Bertha had once explained to her. 'She suffers from an illness which is called migraine.'

'What is migraine?'

'Headaches, but very very bad ones. You and I, we couldn't cope, but your mother is a strong woman, that's why she can go on living. If we suffered the pains she has, our heads would explode.'

'You mean, really explode?' asked Helga, already imagining how Bertha's head would burst in front of her eyes into a thousand pieces of skin and bone. And that was truly a terrifying vision. Bertha without a head, with just a hole on top of her neck where the head should be.

'If your head exploded, would you be dead?' she had asked, little Helga, perhaps five or six years old, having seen Bertha standing in front of her without a head.

'Yes, I would be dead,' replied Bertha as she bent down to the little girl, taking her into her arms.

'We won't die, Helga. Not many people have migraines. And the ones who suffer from them have little helpers who live in the pillbox, little capsules which they swallow and then they feel better.'

'And their heads don't explode?'

'No, they don't explode.'

Since that day Helga has had great respect for the pillbox. When her parents went out in the evening, she used to lie awake in bed, afraid that her mother had forgotten the pillbox. Because what would happen if the migraine started and she didn't have her capsules to help her? Helga imagined little soldiers who, once inside her mother's stomach, would crawl out of the casing and climb up into her mother's head, where they would fight against the migraine, an ugly octopus-like monster. Sometimes the girl became so frightened that she would sneak through the silent house to her mother's room to check. But not once did her mother forget her pillbox. Then Helga grew older and the worry about Mother forgetting her pills diminished and probably also the fear that her head might explode.

Now Helga lies in her bed as if frozen stiff. As if in a dream where you want to run away but can't. Your legs won't move; your whole body won't move. Instead and all of a sudden, warm liquid is running between her legs. Weeing in her bed like a little child. And this is no dream. Helga is awake and has been awake the whole time and she knows now that Mother is standing beside her bed and the box has already made a clicking sound. And tears are streaming from Helga's eyes, running down her cheeks, and wee is flowing between her legs. Warm tears and warm wee run out of her. All warmth runs out of her. And her body lies stiff and motionless, her legs still pressed to her chest, her hands clasped underneath the blanket as if in prayer. She feels movement above her – it's Hilde. The mattress shook.

Then for a moment everything stays still. Dead still. Mother doesn't move.

Helga would love to run – across a meadow, a huge green meadow full of buttercups – run hand in hand with Knut. There she is, running, and the sun is shining and she is laughing and Knut is laughing too. The wind lifts her up and she is now floating on air. Then she hears a click. A metallic sound. And she lies still. In a moment Mother will come and she will fling her arms around Mother's neck and they will sit cuddled up on the bed. Mother will warm her, because Helga is now shivering. Wee is no longer running and has turned cold between her legs. Her shoulder is being touched. Reek of sweat. A sharp, pungent smell. Mother doesn't smell like that. Helga's stomach is about to turn. But then it doesn't. Even this movement is no longer happening. Even her stomach is immobilized. And Helga is gripped by the shoulders and turned on her back. The face of her mother. Mother, Mother. I am so happy! Now every-thing is fine. Helga releases her clasped hands and wants to open her arms to put them around her mother. But her arms aren't moving. Quick, quick, they have to open. But she cannot. Her eyes are still closed too. So she can't have seen the face of her mother! And an ice-cold hand grasps her chin and starts squeezing it. And Helga's head begins to shake; her body begins to shake. And her hands let go of each other, releasing the blanket, blindly fending off the attacker. She is able to move again. It's not Mother; it can't be Mother. Someone wants her life; someone wants to kill her. Scream for help. Scream. She is pulling herself up. She has to get out of this bed. She will run to Father for help. Father! Father! Where are you? The pungent smell of sweat is unbearable. Mother has never stunk like this. Never. Helga must open her eyes. But her eyes don't obey. The rest of her body is now moving, fighting for survival.

Only her eyes! Only her eyes!

Then she forces them open.

And sees the face of her mother. And feels the weight of her mother pushing down on her. And feels the ice-cold hands of her mother on her jaws.

And goes limp.

'Helga, open your mouth.' And hears her mother's voice.

Helga would love to say, 'Mother.' Would love to open her arms. But she trips, stumbles backwards, falls. Into the deep, dark crevasse. She can still see the face of her mother, getting smaller and smaller.

And she opens her mouth to scream.

THE VISION OF
MAGDA GOEBBELS

And while the enemy soldiers amuse themselves with her eldest, so that Magda and her children have enough money to buy stale bread, the small ones loiter on the streets, unkempt, emaciated. It won't be long before they have learnt to steal, perhaps even to kill in order to survive. Meanwhile Magda is lying in a dirty bed infested with bugs, unable to move because of the pain – she can only wait for her daughter to return with the morphine. Despite her youth and beauty, there are days where Helga isn't able to attract enough clients and cannot pay for Magda's drugs. But the rumour has made the rounds of the enemy that this Helga, the one with the dimples and the long legs, is in fact Goebbels's daughter. Yes indeed, Goebbels. There are pigs among the enemy who find this association particularly stimulating and exciting.

Helga is very careful to hide her wounds and bruises. Although it is nearly impossible, as Magda and her six children share a single basement room, where only one tiny barred window above Magda's bed looks onto the pavement outside. Helga tries to conceal her body from her mother, changing in the darkest corner. But sometimes she needs to wash herself and there is only space for the basin right in the middle of the room.

'Mother, turn to the wall,' says Helga.

Magda complies with her daughter's wish – after all, it's the only way she can help her to preserve some of her dignity. Hilde has taken the three little ones to 'school' three roads away, where a couple of older children meet up with younger ones every morning for two hours to practise reading and writing. Hilde has promised her mother she will never tell anyone that they are Goebbels's children.

'Mother, we are not stupid,' Hilde had replied cheekily. 'We don't like stones to be thrown at us, do we? We told them our surname is Schuhmeier.' And with a throaty laugh she had added, 'You are now Frau Schuhmeier,' bending down to her mother and giving her a kiss on the forehead. Then she straightened herself again. 'Have you done your business?'

Since the catastrophe her children have become sober and pragmatic. Magda shook her head.

'No, I can't do it.'

Hilde pulled a disapproving face.

'Mother, this is no good. You need more exercise,' she said, lifting the covers and removing the shallow enamel dish from underneath Magda's behind. She returned her hand underneath the covers to pull down Magda's nightie, an old soldier's shirt which the children had found.

'If you are not feeling too bad tonight, Helmut and I will carry you around the room a bit. But now we have to leave. It's late.'

The four little ones filed beside Magda's bed, each giving their mother a goodbye kiss before leaving the room.

Sometimes the children lift Magda out of bed and try to walk around with her in the room. They worry that otherwise she will develop bedsores. It started with her legs two weeks after the catastrophe. Soon she couldn't move them at all. Since then she has been bedridden. Also, the pain in her face returns more frequently now, the left side already totally numb like back in May '43. The headache is her constant companion. Didn't Doktor Moroll warn her over a year ago that her body wouldn't tolerate further psychological shocks? Magda is dying; she knows it. Do the children know?

Helga feels unobserved. She has stripped naked. The washbasin is filled with water. It is much too small to sit down in. Helga lifts her right leg and rests it on the edge of the basin, bending slightly forward. She wets the flannel in her hand and washes between her legs. Magda lies on her side facing the wall. Slowly she turns her head. Her skull feels as if it is being squeezed in a vice. But she manages to glance over her shoulder. She sees every single rib in her daughter's back moving, so thin and skeletal and transparent has the girl become. She also sees haematomas and bruises and open wounds. Helga is lost in her own thoughts; she doesn't notice how her mother is turning in bed, is sitting up and trying to lift her legs onto the floor. She only hears the clattering noise when Magda falls head first to the floor. The girl jumps, turns around startled, grabbing the towel and holding it in front of her body.

'Mother!'

She takes two steps towards Magda, who lies with her face flat on the ground and doesn't move. She kneels down next to her. She touches her mother's trembling shoulders. Then she hears a sob.

'Did you hurt yourself?'

Magda shakes her head.

'Can you stay like this for a moment? I just want to put on some clothes.'

Magda nods.

Helga puts on the still-damp dress that she had washed and hung to dry over the line strung across the room. She turns her mother carefully onto her side, puts a cushion under her head. Magda's face twitches. Helga, leaning over her, holds her head and whispers soothingly, 'It's all right, everything will be fine, Mother. Don't you worry. Tomorrow I will be able to buy more morphine. I promise.'

Magda's attack lasts a few minutes, then it is over. Her head is now lying in her daughter's lap. Helga has sat down on the floor behind the prone woman. Magda is crying.

'I don't want to take any more from you. No more. Do you understand? I don't want you to go out to earn money any more.'

For a moment Helga doesn't answer. Then she replies calmly, 'I have to earn money, otherwise we will starve.'

'But not like this,' sobs Magda.

Again, silence reigns for a moment.

'That was only one. He will never come back.' Helga's voice is calm.

'What do you mean, he will never come back?'

'The man who did this to me won't ever come back.'

'Did he say that?'

A quick laugh escapes Helga's mouth. 'Of course he didn't say that.'

'So how do you know?'

Helga shrugs her shoulders. 'I know. That's all. Come, I'll help you back into bed.' She gets onto her feet behind her mother, puts her arms under Magda's and links her forearms in front of Magda's chest. Then she lifts Magda's upper body, turns her in a semicircle so that Helga's own back is facing the bed, sits down on the bed and pulls her mother up. Magda is now lying on top of her daughter. Helga wriggles free. She gets up, straightens her mother in the bed, places the pillow under Magda's head, moves her legs next to each other, covers her with the blanket. Magda has closed her eyes. The pain in her head is pounding away. A few minutes later Helga leaves the room, dressed in her work clothes, Magda's old red day-dress, which was in the only suitcase they had taken. At some point Magda hears through a fog of pain Hilde and the little ones returning. She hears Helmut whispering, 'Psst. Mother is asleep. Be quiet.' And she feels Heide's clumsy little hand on her cheek and then feels her climb into bed beside her. Eventually the light is turned off. One of the children always sleeps with her, though not Helga and Hilde, who are too big. Magda lies in the only bed, while the children sleep on mattresses they have found somewhere outside. Dirty, disgusting and smelly. At first Magda had felt revulsion rise from her stomach into her throat.

'What exactly do you want us to do?' Hedda had asked, a seven-year-old who answered her mother back. 'The floor is hard, we prefer to sleep on dirty mattresses.'

For Magda the nights are the best time. The pain is less then, perhaps because she is aware of all her children safe and soundly sleeping with her in the same room. Even Helga doesn't work at night. Up to now Magda has been able to extract this promise from her. There is more drinking in the streets at night, it's worse then. Magda is now completely awake. The window is slightly open. A gentle breeze is blowing into the room and caresses Magda's body. The wind is still mild. But the thought of the approaching winter frightens her. They have no way of heating the room and no warm clothes either. And food will be in even shorter supply. She turns her head slightly to the side and buries her nose in Heide's hair. And despite the dirt, the lice, the decay, she is still able to smell her child. A warm, soft smell mixed with sweat and even urine. A baby or toddler smell. How long will such a smell last? She moves a few inches away from her youngest and pushes her arm gently beneath the child's neck. Then she shuffles closer again, as close as possible towards the child's body, and embraces it with her other arm. She buries her nose once again in the child's hair and now lies totally still, feeling Heide's breathing against her own body, inside her own body. To become one once more with this breathing, the way it used to be. Magda now lives for these moments where she holds a child in her arms. Ideally when they are asleep. Then they are hers one more time. Then she protects their sleep; then nothing else exists outside this room.

She strokes Heide's hair. Matted and dirty. But Magda is no longer disgusted by dirt and filth on the bodies of her children. She no longer minds stroking their filthy hair, kissing it, smelling it. It's still her children's hair. She used to find dirty hair revolting. All the bacteria and diseases that could lurk in there. Scrubbed down, that's what the children had to be, every other day, from head to toe. Only then were they allowed to come into her room and give her a kiss on the forehead, one after the other. More than this she often couldn't manage, the headaches rendering every touch unbearable. But now she is holding this living breathing body in her arms and is simply happy. For a short while, in the middle of the night, she is able to forget everything: the enemy, life outside and what will become of them in the winter when they aren't able to heat the room or find warm clothes.

She told the children to try to get to Schwanenwerder.

'Schwanenwerder no longer exists.' This time it was Helmut, her little frail Helmut, who answered her back. He hadn't worn his Indian headdress for a long time. 'I left it in the bunker,' he explained to his mother, totally composed, when she had asked him if he wasn't the big Indian chief any longer. 'No,' he'd replied, 'Indians don't really exist any more, and anyway they never existed in Germany in the first place.' And now he says Schwanenwerder doesn't exist any more either.

'How do you know that Schwanenwerder no longer exists?' asked Magda.

'Mother, you have no idea how the world looks outside now.' Helmut lowered his voice, leaning closer towards his mother. 'The . . . the enemy has destroyed everything. And if a building is still standing they ransack it first and then they blow it up. Everywhere it's like this. And anyway we are not allowed to leave the city. We have to stay where we are. They've surrounded us. There are barriers all around.'

'What, only around us?'

'No, of course not just around us. Around the whole city. We cannot leave the city.'

'And what about food?'

'We always find something,' Helmut replied. 'We shouldn't worry too much.'

He paused for a moment, then he leant even closer towards his mother, now touching her ear with his lips. Magda felt his breath tickling her ear.

'Helga told us not to call them our enemies any longer.'

'What are we supposed to call them, then?'

'I don't know, but not enemies. She says it's no longer possible that they are our enemies because they are the people we now have to live with.'

What was her daughter talking about? These people, these beasts in human shape, had destroyed the work of the Führer. How could Helga – her Helga, the Führer's Helga, He who had been the first to hold her in His arms, even before Joseph held his daughter, because he had been disappointed that it wasn't a boy – how could this girl betray her Führer, National Socialism, her own beliefs, in such a way? Magda gently stroked Helmut's head, whispering back into his ear, 'I will talk to Helga. They are our enemies, Helmut. You should never forget that. They are not human beings; they only look as if they are.'

'But Helga says they are people just like you and me. And most of them are apparently quite nice. They only want to survive, like we do.'

Magda patted Helmut's cheek. Her arm started trembling again and the pain resonated inside her entire head. She closed her eyes and turned to the wall. When Helga returned later on, she sent the other children out of the room. She didn't want them to listen to their conversation. Magda had managed to sit up, leaning her back against the wall. Helga was sitting at the small rickety wooden table, with her back to her mother, writing. It is the only thing that reminds Magda of her Helga from before, the writing. She is still writing her diary. And always takes it with her out of the room and hides it somewhere outside.

'I have sent the little ones out in order to talk to you,' Magda said.

'I know,' Helga answered without turning around, without ceasing to move her pen across the paper in front of her. Where does she get those new notebooks from? What does she have to do for that? How far does she need to degrade herself for it? Degraded by the enemy. The enemy! Magda took a deep breath. If she started to shout, Helga would simply leave the room. She had done it before. She had power over her mother now and exploited it. Magda could no longer run after her. Could no longer do anything. She could only talk to her child. That was all.

'Please, Helga, I'd like to talk to you.'

'What about?' Helga barked the words out.

'Could you come and sit next to me on the bed?' asked Magda. She could hear herself pleading. It was pathetic.

'Why, Mother? So you can talk to me about the enemy?'

Magda was taken aback. She hadn't expected Helmut to run straight to his sister.

'Well, are you surprised?' Helga had now turned around in the chair and was looking at Magda with open animosity. 'Of course Helmut told me that you think the others are our enemies.'

Helga turned back to her notebook, grabbed her pen and bent low over the table. For a moment there was silence. Magda knew Helga wasn't writing. Her elbows weren't moving. But she also knew that Helga was on the point of storming out of the room. It would only take another word out of turn from her mother. Helga was waiting for it.

'Are these . . . these men nice to you?'

'No. But some pay me.'

'Some?'

'Yes, Mother, some.'

'And you call them our friends?'

'No, I am not calling them our friends. But they tell me that this is what the German soldiers have done to their women – and much worse. And I now have to pay for it. It's that simple. But they let us live.'

Magda's eyes filled with tears. She longed for her daughter to come and sit on the bed. But Helga remained at the table.

'And you believe what they tell you?'

Helga jumped up so suddenly that the chair flew backwards. Magda's entire body tensed.

'Do you actually know what was going on all those years? What the Führer, Father, all of them were doing? Do you really believe that German soldiers raping Russian women was the worst of it?'

Helga's face, contorted with anger, moved close to her mother. Crying now, she grabbed her mother's arm, grasped it so hard that her own hand was burning. She started to shake the bedridden woman, bending over her, gripping the other arm as well, bringing her face right up to her mother's.

'They exterminated people, human beings. And they built huge gas chambers to do it, all over the place. While we were sitting in Schwanenwerder in the garden underneath a blue sky enjoying our plum cake, Father and the Führer gave orders to exterminate humans. Millions. Do you understand? Millions!'

She let go of her mother's arm and turned away, heading towards the door.

'Helga, please don't go.'

Helga had already put a hand on the door handle.

'They are making it up. It's a conspiracy. It's all a big lie. Yes, it is true, some of our enemies had to be punished,' Magda gasped out. 'War is a cruel time, but—'

Helga let go of the door handle, turned around, approaching her mother once more with her hand high in the air. Instinctively, Magda lifted an arm in front of her face for protection.

'Shut up!' Helga screamed. 'Shut up!' Now standing in front of her mother's bed once again, she took a deep breath, lowered her arm.

'No, I won't hit you. No, I won't do that,' she said more calmly now. 'You are suffering enough.'

She paused for a moment before continuing: 'We have lost the war because we had to lose it. Most of the people out there are happy that the war is over. Including the ones who fought against us.'

'And now? What will become of us? We are rotting like rats in a hole.'

'Yes, indeed, but we are alive and perhaps tomorrow it will be better. And I don't ever want to hear you say again that these people out there are our enemies. Enemies don't exist, never existed. You all just imagined them.'

Magda promised Helga never to talk again about the enemy and enemies. What else could she do? Oh, my Führer, what else could I have done? I am too weak, too ill, to protect my children from the enemy. Magda buries her nose even deeper into Heide's hair. She forces herself to breathe calmly and quietly, until she can feel once again Heide's breathing against her own body. She listens to the breathing of the other children. Someone smacks their lips. Who was it? Then she hears a whimper.

'Psst, psst,' she whispers into the darkness.

'Mother?'

'Yes, darling.'

It's Helmut.

'I'm frightened.'

'Come here.'

'Is there room?' Helmut whispers. 'I thought Heide was sleeping in your bed tonight.'

'Yes, but we can all cuddle up close.'

A moment later she feels Helmut climbing over her and Heide, squeezing in next to the wall. Magda pushes Heide's body as close as possible to the edge of the bed. Her own elbow is now hanging in the air, but she holds tightly onto Heide. She turns as much as possible onto her side towards the girl to give Helmut more space. He pushes right against her back.

'You are so nice and warm,' whispers Helmut. And after a while: 'Do you remember, we were never allowed to climb into bed with you – I mean before? Either you were out or you had such headaches. When I had bad dreams, it was only Bertha who came to me and stroked my head. But that's nowhere near as nice as this.'

The boy rubs his nose against his mother's back. A few moments later, his breathing becomes more regular. Magda listens to her children sleeping. She is guarding their sleepy breath. Until tomorrow morning they'll be safe.

THE FINAL TASK

She sits on Helga's bed and can't move. Her legs are shaking, uncontrollably. She has fixed her eyes on the door handle. She has only to get up, take a few steps and she will be at the door, then she can open it. Then she can leave the room. She has to leave this room in order to join Him outside, He who has already been purified by the fire. She grips the edge of the bed with both hands and tries to lift herself up. But her legs won't obey. She doesn't even manage to move them so that the soles of her feet touch the ground. Her shaking legs are stretched out in front of her, heels on the floor. She cannot bend her legs. With both hands she takes hold of her right thigh. If only she managed to stand up on one leg, she could then let herself fall forward, crawling the couple of metres to the door. There she would pull herself up. She is pushing the palms of her hands against the thigh. But she cannot get a grip. Her hands simply lie limp on her trembling leg. She has to wait for the shaking to abate. She closes her eyes, trying to control her breathing. She opens her eyes. She fixes them on the door handle once more. She hasn't covered Helga yet. The others are covered. But not Helga.

A feeling of panic at never being able to leave this room suddenly tightens Magda's throat. She gasps for air. Presses both hands against her chest. Her entire body is now shaking. She still cannot get up. She can no longer breathe. She is gasping for air like a fish on dry land. Oh, my Führer, help me. Why have you forsaken me? Why am I so weak? I am a courageous mother. The Mother of the Nation. Her fingers fondle the gold medal that the Führer has fastened with His own hands to the collar of her jacket. He knew she would follow Him. She will follow Him. With her children. The Führer is waiting for her. She can't disappoint Him. She can't allow herself to faint. She has to reach the door. The door is locked from the inside. She herself locked it. So no one would disturb her, not even Joseph – especially not Joseph.

She rocks back and forth, her legs trembling uncontrollably. She rocks back and forth. A whimpering noise escapes her throat. She tries not to lose sight of the door handle. The only fixed point that now exists. She has to reach it. Again she attempts to put the soles of her feet on the floor. Impossible. She needs to calm down. Needs to think, to work out how to get out of this room. Form a plan. Then she will be able to move. She has thought about everything. Except the aftermath. During their last weeks in Schwanenwerder, how often did she sneak at night into the children's rooms and stand by their beds, looking at them, her sleeping angels, one after the other. She swept their sweaty hair out of their faces, sitting down next to them on their beds to observe them in their sleep, pondering various escape plans. To leave Schwanenwerder in the middle of the night, under cover of darkness. In her mind's eye she saw how she and the children, dressed in rags, would sneak through the forest and jump onto a moving train somewhere. Danger lurked everywhere. Everyone knew their faces from the newsreels. The enemy would be everywhere. They would want to hunt them down. And they wouldn't be the only ones. The common people would desert to the enemy. They wouldn't be safe anywhere.

She had pictured life in a rat hole, a cellar somewhere, surrounded by the enemy, her daughters raped and abused, her son gone mad out of fear. Helmut, who had such a gentle soul. All his life he had imagined enemies at every corner, even in Schwanenwerder, where loyal soldiers had protected them day and night – even there he thought he could see enemies. How would he be able to live among real enemies? His childlike soul wouldn't be able to handle such a collision with reality.

She is rubbing her thigh with the palms of her hands. She is rocking back and forth.

She had pictured life afterwards. She had pictured the deed. But she had never pictured how she would leave the room.

Her throat is burning. The sour taste has settled in her mouth. A cockroach is scuttling into the room from underneath the door, then along the wall, towards the beds of the little ones. Revulsion overcomes her. She gulps for air. She had imagined life afterwards. The cellar, the rat hole where they would rot. The dark, gruesome reality of living with the enemy. She pictured every detail. Her children fending for themselves, with a dying mother dependent on morphine. At the mercy of the enemy. It would have been a matter of time and they all would have died a wretched death one after the other. Crushed like cockroaches. Squashed like insects.

She pictured putting a cyanide capsule into each of her children's mouths. In front of her mind's eye she pushed their jaws together. She hadn't left anything to chance. She had thought everything through. Many times. Visualized it, so that the pictures would eventually take the shock out of the reality. So that she could proceed according to plan. Without thinking. She had decided on the order of the children. First Helmut. The boy had to go first, because with him, whom she had always wanted to protect, who was so gentle and frail, who just wasn't made for this cruel world, with him she would find it the most difficult. She knew, once he had gone, she would have no choice but to send the girls after him. Heide would be the next after Helmut. And then the other girls according to age, with Helga last. She had entered the room and proceeded as planned. She had acted in accordance with the pictures in her head. Mentally ticking them off. She is an obedient girl. She is the woman at His side. Once more she feels for the gold medal. His gold medal. Like a wedding ring. He has married the mother of His children. My Führer, give me strength!

And as her fingers touch the medal she suddenly feels something soft in the breast pocket of her jacket. She lets go of the medal, puts her fingers inside the pocket and pulls out six little white bows.

At once the shaking stops. She has to fasten a bow into

each of her children's hair. A symbol of innocence. A symbol of their holiness. How did she forget. She has to follow her plan step by step – only then will she succeed. Everything has its place, everything has meaning. She has to obey the plan. As He fastened the gold medal to her jacket, so she must fasten the white ribbons to her children's hair. She rises to her feet.

Standing in the middle of the room, she opens her arms wide. A mighty goddess. She will gather her children and take them back down into the blackest darkness where she will await her time. They will return to the darkness from whence they came. When mankind has progressed and is able to handle what they have to offer, they will come back. The day will come when He will summon her once more, of that she is sure. He will call her and she will rise from the dead and return to the kingdom of the living. And she will bring with her her children, garbed in pure innocence. She turns and moves from one child to the next, kissing them on their foreheads, as they stand at the gates of His kingdom.

She sits down next to her youngest, little Heide. Gently she brushes the hair out of the pale child's face. Heide's mouth is slightly open, a soft round mouth, not yet completely weaned off the bottle. Luckily this child will never know a life without Him. Stroking the soft blonde hair, she grasps a little bunch at the top of Heide's head and ties round the white ribbon. Very soon the word Nazi will become a swearword. It will be synonymous with war and annihilation. People will forget how the world looked before Him. How poverty, desperation, meaninglessness, rootlessness had taken hold. People will drag the word through the mud, those barbarians above Magda who are already raping women and children and killing old people. A horde of drunken, bloodthirsty barbarians is roaming above her – Stone Age creatures, without words, without education, without culture.

He recognized the world for what it is and moulded it according to His vision. He attempted to bring beauty to mankind. But they fought against Him, made fun of Him, for a long time did not take Him seriously. He had to prove to them how determined He was. Magda's eyes fill with tears. She is now standing beside the second child. She is stroking Hedda's head one last time before she ties the ribbon into the girl's hair. He was the first unapproachable man, one who didn't know any lust, who saw her, Magda, as a human being, who saw all women as human beings, not existing for the satisfaction of men but essential to the rebirth of the nation. He put procreation and physical intimacy in their places. He assigned to the body the minor role it deserves in a highly developed, cultured society.

The third child, Holde. Carefully Magda unfastens her two plaits, arranging the loose hair around her sweet face. Then she takes a few strands of hair from the girl's middle parting to tie the third ribbon.

For a moment she stands by Helmut's bed, looking down at him, transfixed by utter tenderness. Here they are in a cave – they, the last survivors, have withdrawn into a cave. Through Him the human race was given hope once more. But mankind doesn't progress, doesn't want to progress. There they are in the valleys, huddled around open fires, carving axes out of wood. And when someone comes down from the mountain to proclaim their salvation, they don't want to hear; they cannot hear. They close their eyes and ears, and accuse him of murder.

Magda lifts her right arm, stretches it out. 'Heil Hitler,' she whispers, sobbing. She knows what the others think; she's heard them talking, the other women. They won't harm us; we are innocent and our children too. Innocent? Why innocent? Why guilty? In these two words alone lies their betrayal. They are traitors, all of them; they never really believed in Him and His vision. They jumped on the bandwagon, because they thought it would be to their advantage, providing them with a nice, pleasant life. They never cared about Him; they never cared for His vision. Now the enemy is approaching and they lie down in submission.

She bends over her son and fastens a ribbon. It takes a bit longer because of his short hair.

She is a courageous mother; her angels will one day be worshipped as saints. She is a bringer of symbols, six angels in white tunics who have fallen asleep, slipped away from this world of decay and destruction. Slipped away because the world didn't deserve them, couldn't appreciate their purity. The cruelty of the enemy has robbed these pure creatures of the air that they breathe.

Hilde's eyes are open. Magda flinches briefly, but then strokes Hilde's face with the palm of her hand and closes the eyes. Hilde has the most beautiful hair of all, soft and charmingly wavy. The little ribbon complements her looks in the most delightful way.

And Magda imagines six little carved white marble coffins on the shoulders of men in uniform, the mourning masses lining the route of the cortège, throwing flowers and wreaths and shedding tears. Then the crowd falls on its knees and swears to avenge this innocence, this purity that has had to give way to chaos once again. Her children will become a symbol of the fragility of His premature vision. They will become a symbol of hope. Hope that when next time a pure genius emerges from the masses, this childish innocence will have matured, become strong enough to take up the fight. And she, Magda, will live on; this act will immortalize her in the memory of the people. It will take time. Him, her and their six children. Men will fall onto their knees in front of the blessed couple who will give them courage and perseverance and faith. And they will profess gratitude to her, gratitude for her boundless loyalty to Him and for not abandoning her children to the enemy.

She is now leaning down towards Helga. Her darling girl. How beautiful she is! Her hair spread out on the pillow. She takes a loose strand and ties the final white bow. Her little saint. She pulls the grey blanket over Helga's shoulders.

Outside the door Joseph is pacing up and down.

'Why did it take so long? I almost came in.'

She had told him not to come in. He couldn't have coped with the sight. Joseph doesn't understand that these children aren't his. And she and her children will rise again. Joseph's task is completed.

'Can I see them?'

'No, you can't.'

They are not his children and they have now entered His kingdom. His Third Reich that will last far more than a thousand years. She feels sorry for Joseph. He suddenly appears small and helpless.

'Your task is completed.'

She places her hand on his forearm soothingly.

'We have to go now.'

'Magda, I have to see my children one last time.'

'Your task is completed,' she repeats. She wants to add, and His and my task is just beginning.

But He wouldn't understand that either.

'It's OK, Joseph. Let's go now.'

He doesn't move, staring at the door, his lower lip trembling, tears in his eyes.

'Please,' he now begs, helplessly.

Can't he manage the last step?

'Think about Him,' she hisses. 'He went before us. Do you want to disappoint Him?'

Joseph suddenly turns to confront her, fixing her with his piercing dark eyes.

'What are you saying? You are telling me that I deceived Him? I, the most loyal of all His followers?'

'Pull yourself together.' She hears the singing of drunken soldiers.

'I can't leave without giving my children one last kiss.'

She shakes her head. 'We have to hurry. We don't have much time left.'

He doesn't move.

'Pull yourself together,' she whispers again. He behaves

like a common man. One of them. 'We have a task to under-take.'

A drunken soldier staggers by. 'Heil Hitler!'

She turns around and heads towards the staircase. Joseph follows. They climb the narrow concrete steps. Magda's fingers are scraping along the rough grey wall. Then she slides a hand into her skirt pocket, her thumb pushes down the lever, she feels the lid jump open. She keeps on climbing and lifts her head and sees a ray of light at the top. And she lifts her hand out of the pocket to her mouth and places the last capsule under her tongue. And she takes one last step and walks into the light.

AFTERWORD

Magda is a portrayal of a destructive mother–daughter relationship over three generations. My aim was not to provide an historically accurate account but to capture the psychology of the characters. I have used fact and fiction as necessity dictated.

MEIKE ZIERVOGEL